T0367509

# Unimaginable

*a novel*

SHALENE SHELLENBARGER

ARCHWAY
PUBLISHING

Archway Publishing books may be ordered through booksellers or by contacting:

Archway Publishing
1663 Liberty Drive
Bloomington, IN 47403
www.archwaypublishing.com
1 (888) 242-5904

Because of the dynamic nature of the Internet, any web addresses or links contained in this book may have changed since publication and may no longer be valid. The views expressed in this work are solely those of the author and do not necessarily reflect the views of the publisher, and the publisher hereby disclaims any responsibility for them.

Any people depicted in stock imagery provided by Thinkstock are models, and such images are being used for illustrative purposes only. Certain stock imagery © Thinkstock.

ISBN: 978-1-4808-1970-2 (sc)
ISBN: 978-1-4808-1971-9 (e)

Library of Congress Control Number: 2015909981

Print information available on the last page.

Archway Publishing rev. date: 07/01/2015

# CHAPTER ONE

Summer 1997

I was sleeping when there was a knock on the door. I thought it was strange, because my room was upstairs and I had never heard someone knock on the door before. It was loud. I looked over toward my nightstand to see what time it was. The alarm clock said 7:18 A.M, I recalled with a vivid memory. It was a gift from my mom for my seventh birthday. She said that I could have one since I was a big girl now and it was time that I wake up on my own. Of course, it took a few days for me to understand what "A.M. and P.M." meant.

I got out of bed to see who was knocking on the door and stubbed my toe on the bed frame. I stumbled down the stairs with tears in my eyes. As I got to the last step, I saw my father crumpling to the floor in front of the door. I'd heard him yelling, but could not understand what he was saying.

The sun coming in through the door silhouetted the police officer standing there with his hat being held in his hands. He looked very upset. He looked at me as I approached them. Something was really wrong with my dad.

"Daddy, what's wrong?" He didn't answer me. A crumbled mass in the doorway, he kept rocking, shaking his head, mumbling to himself.

"This can't be. This cannot be happening to us." He repeated the words over and over. "No. You must be mistaken. It can't be her. I just talked to her an hour ago."

*Who did he just talk to?* I looked around, trying to see if someone else was in the room I hadn't seen. There was no one else. What can't be happening? He wasn't making any sense to my young brain. I sat down beside him and put my hand on his shoulder. He shrugged it off, and shook his head. That really hurt my feelings. I started to cry a little. He was beginning to scare me.

My daddy had never scared me before, except for the time I broke a bunch of eggs on the kitchen floor when I was five. I was trying to make breakfast for Mommy and him, but I couldn't figure out how to turn on the stove. Instead, Daddy came downstairs to a big, huge mess. He was not happy at all. I was grounded for a whole week.

The officer, who was standing outside when I walked down stairs, looked up at me with sadness in his eyes. "What's your name sweetie?"

I looked at him for a few minutes. Hesitantly, I finally decided I should tell him.

"Angel Elizabeth Brady." I didn't like strangers. Mommy always told me not to talk to strangers, so I never did. She said I was very smart for my age and she didn't have to worry about whether or not I could tell if someone was a stranger. I didn't care if this person was in a policeman uniform. He was still a stranger who did something to make my daddy very sad.

The officer walked past my father and knelt down so he was at eye level with me. He smiled, his white teeth barely showing. "It's nice to meet you. I'm Officer Raider. I know you're probably not supposed to talk to strangers, but now we aren't strangers, right?" He waited for me to answer. I nodded. "How old are you Angel?"

"Seven and a half." I started to twirl my red, curly hair around my finger. This was a nervous habit I had picked up when kindergarten started. I was really scared to go to kindergarten and leave my mommy home by herself. She cried when she took me to school the first day, so I worried about her all day.

"What's wrong with my daddy? Why did you make him cry?" I asked accusingly. The officer looked back over his shoulder, at my father, who was still rocking and mumbling things I could not understand.

"Do you have someone you want me to call to come and help with your daughter, Mr. Brady?" He received no answer, so he shook his head and looked back at me. "Sweetie, where do you go when mommy and daddy go to work?"

After I had decided this man wasn't a stranger any longer, I took his hand and led him to the kitchen where my mom had all the emergency numbers listed. "I go to Grandma Jane's house. She gives me cookies and milk and we watch T.V. and play games." I was getting excited just thinking about going to see her.

"Mr. Brady," Officer Raider called out, "I'm going to call your mother to come and get Angel."

"Fine, fine. Get her out of here," my father screamed from the other room. "I can't deal with her right now, anyway... Oh my God, how am I going to live without my wife? She is the one to handle these things, not me. I can't live without her."

I didn't understand why he would say that. Why would he have to live without Mommy? As I started to put what he was saying together, I looked at Officer Raider.

"What's wrong with my daddy? Why is he talking like that? Where's my mommy? Why do we need to call Grandma?" I was doing what my parents hated. I was asking a million questions.

How else was I supposed to get the answers I wanted? Officer Raider looked down at me with tears in his eyes. He looked back at my dad for a second, then back to me. He crouched down so he was closer to my height.

"Sweetie, your mommy has been in a car accident on her way to work."

"Is she in the hospital? Is she okay? We should go see her because she doesn't like to be alone. She might be scared." My innocence was blind and there was nothing to prepare me for what was coming next.

He hesitated for a second. "No, Angel, we can't go see her. She's not okay. Your mommy was hurt too bad. She's…"

"SHE'S DEAD, ANGEL! SHE'S DEAD! YOU'RE NEVER GOING TO SEE HER AGAIN!" My father stood in the kitchen doorway. Why was he yelling at me? I didn't do anything wrong. He looked really scary. I started to cry again. Officer Raider took me outside. He had called my grandmother who said she was on her way to pick me up. I just wanted my mommy. I couldn't get it through my head — I wasn't going to see her, ever again.

As we were standing outside, I noticed it was really chilly. I started to shiver and the officer gave me his jacket to wear. It was huge on me, but it warmed me. He stood beside me, with his arm wrapped around my shoulders, while we waited.

I heard Grandma pull onto our street. She barely got the car stopped before she jumped out and grabbed me in her arms. She smelled like cherry jelly beans. I buried my tear-streaked face in her shirt and she just held me while I cried. After a few minutes, she focused her attention on the officer.

"Where's Ryan? He can't be handling this well at all. Alisa was his whole life." She was crying, too, which made me cry even harder. I had never seen my grandma cry before. She was always happy.

"Ma'am, he isn't doing well at all. He's not making much sense and doesn't seem to want Angel around him," Officer Raider replied. He whispered the part about me. I didn't think he wanted me to hear what he was saying to Grandma, but I had good ears.

BAM!

It was the loudest bang in my entire life. I jumped so high the jacket I was wearing fell off onto the ground. Grandma screamed and the officer grabbed the gun out of his holster.

"Stay there!" he shouted to Grandma and me as he ran toward the house. My grandma bent down and grabbed the jacket, putting it back over my shoulders. I was shivering so much from fear, Grandma must have thought I was getting cold again.

"It's okay sweetie. You're okay." She squeezed me tighter and patted my head. Grandma started to cry, again. I could feel her shaking.

"What was that noise, Grandma? It was so loud."

"I'm not quite sure, honey, but everything is going to be alright." She stroked my head, pulling the curls with her finger.

A few minutes later, Officer Raider came outside with his hat in his hands, head down. When he looked up at my grandma, she began to cry harder.

"I'm so sorry, Mrs. Brady. Your son has just taken his own life." The words were slow and calm.

What did that mean? He took his own life?

"Oh, no… Oh, no, no, no…" Grandma cried, her knees bent and we both went down to the ground. She held and rocked me there on the driveway. I don't even know how long we sat there.

I didn't really know what all this meant at the young age of seven, but I had become an orphan in less than an hour. One minute, my mommy and daddy were kissing me goodnight, and then the next, they were both gone forever.

The funerals were a few days later. Grandma decided to hold

both together. She said it was because my parents were so in love. She thought it only made sense they be put to rest at the same time.

I remember thinking, if love meant you were going to die, then I didn't want any part of it. It seemed to me love made things painful.

# CHAPTER TWO

Present day

"You are such a goodie-goodie, Angel!" My best friend, Shelly, stomped her feet. It was like watching a two year old child throw a fit. She wanted me to go to a new club that had just opened. "Come on!"

Shelly was the picture perfect bombshell: Long, blonde hair; DD's; and legs that went on forever. In her five inch heels, she towered over me. I was only five-feet two-inches tall when I stretched to my highest. We were complete opposites; her with the model face and figure, and me with my auburn hair and freckles. She has dark brown eyes, where mine are blue-green. I was average, weighing in at 115 pounds. My eyes were what I thought of as my best feature.

"I am not a goodie-goodie. I have this term paper due in two days, Shelly." Yes, I am the definition of a procrastinator. I had started to type said term paper about two hours ago, even though I've known about it for over a month. I was freaking out, even though I already had over half of it done.

Shelly stood with one hand on her hip, the other hand with

and extended finger shaking at me. "You know damned well you will have that paper done in three hours, tops. There is no reason why you can't come out with me tonight. It's just one night. Come on Angel! You don't get out enough. You need to let yourself go and have some fun every now and then." glared at me. "All work and no play makes Angel a very dull girl." Now she was mocking me. I could feel my cheeks heat up.

"UGH!" I slammed the pencil down on my notes. "You're not going to leave me alone unless I go with you, are you? You know the club scene is so not my thing, Shell. There is nothing there that even remotely interests me." I was already shutting off my laptop and putting it away. I knew there was no getting out of this. Once Shelly gets something in that pretty little head of hers, there's no changing her mind. I hope she doesn't mind me going to this club in jeans and a hooded sweatshirt.

"How do you know?" Shelly shrugged. "When was the last time you have been to a bar, let alone an actual club? Maybe you'll finally get laid and clean out those cobwebs in your panties." She laughed as she ran out of my room to escape the pillow I threw . She peeked back in. "Oh and I already have the perfect outfit picked out for you. It's hanging in the bathroom. Hurry up and get a shower so I can do something with your hair!" She was gone.

I sighed as I drug myself to the bathroom. One of these days, I was going to have to tell her 'no', just to see her reaction. I imagine it wouldn't go over very well. She was used to getting her way.

When I turned on the bathroom light, I stopped dead in my tracks at the sight of what was hanging in front of me. Shelly's idea of the perfect outfit for me was a scrap of black fabric I assumed to be a dress. Under where it was hanging, was a pair of black four-inch stilettos. No way. Absolutely not. I shook my head as I undressed and stepped into the shower.

Shelly was right. I probably am a very boring person, I thought as I washed my face. Between my serving job at the local diner, and being in my Junior year of college, I really didn't have the time to do much of anything else. I was working on my Master's degree in Psychology. Ever since I was old enough to understand what had happened with my parents, I decided to find out why my dad decided death was a better option than raising me. I hadn't figured that out, but the thought of helping someone else always interested me. There's just something about picking apart someone's brain…

I quickly shaved my legs, washed up, and stepped out of the shower. I dried off, and glared at the slip of a dress hanging in front of me. It would have looked great on Shelly, but I was definitely too short, and too modest to wear something like that.

"There's no way I am wearing you alone," I said to the dress. It was as if it were there, mocking me. I decided I would wear the dress, as a shirt, along with the new jeans I had bought yesterday. As for the shoes my best friend so sweetly put out for me— Nope, wasn't happening. Instead, I threw them out into the hallway and grabbed a pair of black flats out of my closet. As I put them on, I decided they were a much better fit with my outfit. I refused to break an ankle, or my neck, tonight. If I'm being forced to go out, especially when I have a paper to write, then I am going to be somewhat comfortable. Plus, I needed all of my bones to stay safely in one piece.

I have never been one to put much make-up on. Just the basics: some foundation, powder, eyeliner, and mascara. My hair was in a ponytail. I guess one could say I am kind of a "home body" or "plain Jane." I've been told I'm plain too many times to count. I heard footsteps getting closer. Shelly came into my bedroom and squealed.

"OH MY GOD, Ang! You look hot!" She stood there, hand to chin appraising me. " I really like what you did with the dress.

I knew it was far-fetched for me think you might actually wear it." She looked down at my feet. "So... No heels, huh?"

"Seriously?" I stared at her. I finally noticed her fighting a smile. My attitude changed. "You know me better than that."

"Okay, okay..." she grumbled and reached out to take a strand of my hair in between her fingers. "What should we do with your hair? I don't understand why you always wear it up. It's so pretty. Hmmm.... Oh! I have an idea." She pulled me to the bathroom, shoved me onto the toilet, and went to work. She used the curling iron, pins, hairspray, and who knows what else on my poor head. It was going to take forever to get all of these products out of my hair.

Shelly decided I didn't have enough makeup on and put something on my eyelids and applied more mascara. She put some lip gloss on me, grabbed a pair of earrings and handed them to me. I put them in and she stepped back to look at her finished work.

"You are so beautiful, Angel. You should do something with yourself every now and then, so everyone else can see it, too." She cocked an eye and looked thoughtfully at me . "Oh wait, never mind. You would have to actually get your nose out of the books and leave the apartment for that to happen." She stuck her tongue out at me. I glared back at her before turning to see what she did to me. I had better not look like a damn whore.

"I probably look like a clown or a hooker... Whoa! What did you do to me? Who is that chick?" I didn't recognize the girl looking back at me from the mirror. Who'd have thought? I inspected my reflection. I can clean up nice.

"Let's go! It's already past ten and there's going to be a line all the way around the building. I wanted to be there by now." Shelly was always impatient, as if she was going to miss something important. I reached into my purse, making sure I had my ID, some cash, and my cell phone. Like a breeze, we were out the door, heading for her car.

About twenty minutes later, we parked across the street from a huge building with a bright, neon sign that read "FOREVER 'IT' CLUB." What in the hell did that mean? Kind of conceited if you ask me. How did they know they were going to be there forever? Or if they were even it? I had to stop being so judgmental. I was already hating this place, and we hadn't even been inside yet.

As we approached the huge building, I wondered about Shelly's sanity. What was it she was so worried about us missing? There was definitely not a line going around the building. There were maybe thirty people waiting at the door to get in. The women were dressed like sluts, and the men had 'douche bag' written all over them. Ugh... I hated this place. Shelly is lucky I love her. Otherwise, I wouldn't be caught dead anywhere near this place, let alone inside.

She, of course, immediately dragged me to the bar so we could order our drinks. I bought a beer, and she got a Long Island, along with a shot. She wasn't messing around tonight. I surveyed the building. It was pretty nice, as you could tell it was newly renovated. It was modern, with tall ceilings, and white walls. There was a raised dance floor, with the DJ booth being hidden somewhere in the wall above our heads. The music was interesting, not the stuff I normally listened to, but a little heavier. It, of course, wasn't the scariest I've heard. Attached to the dance floor was another room. It was dark. There must have been a black light in there, because I could see glowing items moving around beyond the doorway. I had to admit this place was clean, and not some hole in the wall bar. It even smelled clean. There was no smoke hovering in the air, no nasty smell of body odor coming from too many sweaty bodies. I had to give Shelly credit.

Shelly immediately grabbed my arm and pulled me toward the dance floor. This girl should know me better. I don't dance unless I have at least three drinks in me. Even then, I'm not sure what I do would actually considered dancing. Instead of arguing with her, I followed toward the loud music. I glanced at the other people on the dance floor. They weren't really dancing, either. They were more or less just swaying. I found that very odd.

Shelly turned many heads, male and female, as we walked to the dance floor. The women were jealous, they wanted to be her. The men wanted to be with her. She never noticed all of the attention. She started dancing right away, whereas I was more or less swaying to the music, like everyone else. She had her own rhythm. Like a magnet, two guys walked up and started dancing with us. Shelly got cozy with the one guy right away. She winked at me over his shoulder and nodded her head at the one who was attempting dance with me. I wasn't feeling it with him, so I just shook my head, excused myself, and headed toward the bathroom. Inside, I walked to the sink to wash my hands. I basically was just trying to escape the noise, and my new admirer.

I looked in the mirror, fixed my lip gloss, and fluffed my hair, not that it had moved at all. When I finished, I walked out, dreading the inevitable. I jumped. The guy was waiting for me, right outside of the door. I hadn't realized he followed me, which kind of freaked me out. Do men not take hints anymore? Maybe I was being paranoid. Either way, this one gave off a very bad vibe. I looked away, hoping he would leave me alone. No such luck.

"Hey," he said as I neared him My intention was to walk by and ignore him. However, I didn't want to come off as a complete paranoid bitch, so I stopped and put on a small smile. He wasn't a bad looking man. He was about four inches taller than me and was well built. I could see his pectoral muscles and a six pack through his somewhat too fitting t-shirt. He had blonde hair and hazel eyes. Nothing really stood out to me as sexy, but he was cute. I guess I could be nice and chat with him for a second like a normal person, instead of running away again.

"Hello." It wasn't original but it was all I could think of to say. He smiled, as if victorious, and led me to an open table near the dance floor. I could keep an eye on Shelly with her new toy. She was on, probably, her fourth drink and I could tell she was feeling pretty good. She was leaning on the big man, like he was her life line. He seemed to be enjoying every moment of it. Of course he was. Any man in his right mind would love to have someone like Shelly all over him.

"So… Yeah…Umm… I'm Ben. What's your name?" The guy sitting with me interrupted my thoughts of how drunk Shelly can get, and the bad decisions she would likely make tonight. I was annoyed, but I attempted to give Ben a chance.

"Angel. Nice to meet you." I gave him my hand to shake. Instead, he brought it to his lips and kissed it. What the Hell? Great… This guy thinks he's smooth, I thought as I pulled my hand away and wiped it on my jeans. I couldn't do this. He was kind of creepy. I looked over at Shelly who was stumbling. I don't think she had more than a few drinks and a shot. I knew Shelly very well —she could handle her alcohol. She out of character, even for a drunk Shelly. She was having a good time, now she appeared very confused and nervous.

It was then that I noticed the guy she was dancing with had his hand up her shirt.

*Asshole!*

Take advantage of a drunk girl. Well, he wasn't getting lucky tonight, at least not with my best friend. I started to get up and tell him exactly that when Ben grabbed my arm.

"Where are you going? We were just getting to know each other. You want to get out of here and find some place quieter to talk?" His words came in rapid fire. He was acting weird now. Alright, buddy, I thought, you have gone too far. You're getting grabby with the wrong female. I yanked my arm away and scowled. It was a look making him shrink down into his seat. Did I have "slut" written on my forehead? I never gave him the idea he had a chance in Hell with me going home with him. I guess being nice was all he needed to have those thoughts in his head.

"I'm going to go get my friend. She has had too much to drink. Plus your friend seems to think that means she wants to have sex with him on the dance floor."

"Aw, come on, leave them alone. She looks like she's having a good time," he whined as he followed me. I looked back at him with disbelief, shook my head, and continued on my trek to my best friend. As I reached her, she looked at me, smiled, and then hugged me, following that with a sloppy kiss right on my lips. This is definitely not the Shelly I knew, and I needed to get her out of here. I looked at her with astonishment.

"I love you, Angel!" she yelled over the loud music. "I'm so glad you came here with me. Isn't this place great?" She stumbled at that moment. It took everything in me to hold her up . This was going to be an interesting drive home.

"I think it's time to go, Shell. You've had way too much to drink I guided her to the exit. She kicked off her heals, bent over to pick them up, stumbled and almost ended up on her face. She giggled. I grabbed her shoes from the floor and yanked her toward the door..

"Hey, where are you going? We were having fun before you showed up." The guy Shelly was dancing with grabbed me. I stopped to glare at him. Great... He's pissedHis red face has sweat rolling down his cheeks. Tattoos covered both arms. I was a little bit intimidated by this guy. Actually, I was very intimidated by him. He was huge. He was at least six-foot-five and weighed probably 250 pounds. I wasn't fighting this one off with a mean look, I thought.

"I could see how much fun you were having with a girl who

is too drunk to even stand up by herself, dude," I said as firmly as I could. Shelly giggled. "Look, it really is time for us to go home. She has to work in the morning and I have a term paper to write." I back and forth between the goliath of a man and Ben. I softened my tone so I didn't seem threatening. "We really need to get going. Thanks for the dances though. It was a good time. Maybe we'll see you guys again sometime," I called over my shoulder and rushed away. We made it to the exit door and Shelly started giggling.

"You sure told them, Angel," she slurred as we staggered our way to her car. I opened her purse and fished for her keys as we approached the car. She must have packed her entire wardrobe in this thing, I thought. I found her keys as we arrived at the car. I heard footsteps behind us. My heart pounded, and the hair on the back of my neck stood on end.

Before I could turn to see who it was, or even think, something hard came out of nowhere. I felt a stabbing pain in my head. As the world went black, I heard Shelly scream.

# CHAPTER THREE

"Angel, wake up. Wake up sweetie. Angel honey, you have to wake up, right now. WAKE UP!" My mom's voice yelled at me. Every time I found myself in a bad dream, Mom would appear and make me wake up. For the last eighteen years, ever since that deadly car accident, she has protected.

I tried to open my eyes, but I there was a blinding pain in my head. I couldn't wake up. Maybe if I could go back to sleep, then I wouldn't hurt anymore. The realization of the events of the club hit me. This wasn't a nightmare where I could wake up. Mom wasn't helping me through this one. My eyes shot open. I tried to get up. Something was holding me down. Where am I? What time is it? I attempted to look around, and through hazy eyes, I saw a little sliver of sunlight coming through a window. Everything hurt. I looked at my hands. They were tied to a headboard. Allowing my eyes adjust to the pain in my head, and the bad lighting, I realized I was in a motel room. A cheap motel room, at that. The walls were yellowed with smoke, and there was dust on every surface. There was an old box television set sitting on top of a dresser, in front of the bed. What is going on? Where is Shelly?

"Shelly?" Silence. "Hello? Can anyone hear me?" Still nothing.

I paniced, which only caused my head to hurt even more. I took some breaths and forced myself to calm down. A sound. At the door. It was the door handle. My heart thudded in my chest. Panic again. Anyone could be walking through that door. I was tied up, it couldn't be a good. There was blinding light as the door opened and the sun shone in. I had to squint to see anything. Even then, I could only make out the silhouette of someone very large in the doorway.

"Who are you? Where's Shelly? What do you want with us?" It was a barrage of questions in one breath.

"Shut up, bitch. You'll see soon enough what we want with you. Actually, we didn't want you at all. We were just trying to keep you busy so we could get to your friend. If you would've just left her alone…" I knew that voice. It was the guy who Shelly was dancing with at the club! He kidnapped us! But why would he do that? He came into the room and closed the door.

"Is Shelly okay? What did you do with her? I swear, if you hurt her… I'll…" Every worst case scenario was playing in my head. I imagined everything horrible happening to my best friend. I began to cry. I was afraid, angry, and in pain, all at the same time.

"You'll what? What could you possibly do to me? You're not in any position to be threatening me." He laughed and came closer. "Your friend is fine. She's sleeping off the drugs I put in her drinks last night. I need her to be lively and energetic. I have a client coming to check her out in a couple of hours." He paused and gave me a curious look. "You on the other hand… Well, I'm not sure what I'm going to do with you."

He grabbed my chin and got really close, as if to inspect me. I almost gagged on the smell of his cigarette-laden breath. He shoved my face really hard, and I fell back onto the bed, the pain in my head overtaking the panic. He shook his head as he ran his hand through is long, black, greasy hair. I'm not sure what Shelly saw in him in the first place. I knew she always has been drawn to the 'bad boy' type, but this guy was just dirty.

"Ben should've taken care of you last night. If he would have done his job, you wouldn't even be a problem right now. I swear there's something wrong with that boy," he Mumbled. So Ben's job was to what? Kill me? Or just keep my busy while this big oaf took off with Shelly? I knew one thing, though. I wasn't about to ask him.

Even with the relief of knowing Shelly was okay, I could feel the ache of tears. I forced them down. I had to try my hardest to keep my composure if there was going to be even the slightest chance of me getting out of this alive. Right now, it wasn't looking good for me.

"Please, let us go. We won't tell anyone anything. I mean, I don't even know where we are. Just let us go. We will find our way home." I didn't like feeling so weak, but I was willing to beg. I didn't know what else to do at this point. I was completely helpless, tied up and not knowing where I was, or where Shelly was. He laughed, a beyond evil laugh, and shook his head.

"You're not going anywhere sweetheart." He turned and went back out the door. I screamed in frustration. The door slammed open and he charged back in, cursing. He grabbed something from his pocket and shoved it in my mouth, gagging me . My mouth was dry, and whatever he stuffed in it made it worse. Tears welled up and I felt one trickle down my cheek.

"I thought you'd be smarter than that. I guess I was wrong, huh, college girl?"

How did he know I was in college? I forgot I had told them I had a paper to write. I looked away from him and closed my eyes, defeated. I had never felt so alone. Please let Shelly be alright, I prayed. That was the last thought on my mind as he walked out of the room again.

I must have dozed off, because when the door opened, it made me jump. There was no light coming in this time, so I figured it must be night again. I closed my eyes quickly, heart pounding. If he thinks I'm asleep, then maybe he'll just leave me alone. I wished, at that moment, I was a better actress. If I could play dead, maybe he would go away and not come back.

I lay there, silent, and felt the bed dip down. The bedside lamp switched on. I felt a cold, wet, fabric pressed gingerly to my head and face. I was confused. This couldn't be the same person who was here earlier. Someone was cleaning me up. I opened my eyes a little and saw it was Ben, the guy who tried so hard to talk to me at the club. I was glad now that I wasn't the bitch to him I wanted to be last night. He pulled the gag out.

"What are you doing?" I croaked as he gently dabbed my face with the cloth. He looked so torn. I could see in his eyes he wasn't comfortable with this turn of events. "Ben, please, tell me what's going on." Maybe I could talk him into letting me out of here. Maybe I could actually use my psychology degree for something other than a framed piece of paper decorating my wall.

"Angel, I wish you would have just stayed at the table with me last night. This wouldn't even be an issue. You wouldn't be here, all bloodied up." He got up and the light hit his face just right. I noticed he had a black eye, and his bottom lip was swollen. He'd been in a fight. I wondered if the other guy had done that to him since he seemed pretty mad at Ben earlier.

"Now I have to figure out what to do with you. Abe doesn't think any of his clients will be interested in you. I don't understand that. I think you're hot. He could easily get a pretty penny for you. I think he's just pissed off. He wants me to kill you, Angel. I don't want to, but I don't know what else to do. I'm pretty sure I won't be able to talk him into anything else. He's already mad at me."

"What clients? That other guy said something about a client coming to look at Shelly. What are you guys doing? Selling girls?"

felt the panic build with the thought of poor Shelly being sold as a sex slave to some creepy old man. My mind played out scenes of her being tied up, like I was right now, or being tortured. I mean, anyone who would buy a woman couldn't be a normal human being, could he? He would more likely be into torture, like whips and chains. I paused as the one thought seared through my mind. Rape! I shuddered.

Ben stood there, silently, watching me. I'm sure he could see I was starting to really freak out. He didn't deny what I accused him of, so I gathered I must have been right. I would rather die myself, than to have to go through something like that, or have poor Shelly endure it. I had to get us out of here—fast. Somewhere safe and far away from these crazy people.

I remembered Abe, as Ben called him, saying he had a client coming in a couple of hours. Was Shelly already gone? I had no idea how long I had been asleep before Ben came in. Shit. What would I do if she was already too far away, and it was too late to save her?

"Where's Shelly, Ben?" I looked him directly in the eyes. I needed to at least attempt to stay level headed, if for no other reason than to get information. "Have you guys hurt her?"

"She's being cleaned up." Ben glanced at the curtained window. "She hasn't been harmed. This client doesn't like his girls to be marked up when he gets them." He exhaled a deep breath. "He would be pissed if she was hurt." he said.

Okay, so I have time. Very little time. This was all just so foreign to me. I wasn't so innocent that I didn't' know human trafficking existed. What I didn't know—it had made its way into my neighborhood. I had to think of something fast. An idea formed. If I could get Ben to let me use the bathroom, I could escape through a window. I only had one chance at this, so I had to make it work.

"Ben, I need to use the bathroom." I nodded toward the toilet. "Also, I'm extremely thirsty. Whatever Abe put in my mouth has really dried me out."

He hesitated for a minute. I held my breath. I was beginning to think he was going to say no when he interrupted my thoughts.

"Okay, but you have to be quiet. Abe would kill me if he knew I let you out of this bed." Ben shrugged. "He would probably kill me just for talking to you." He started to untie my hands., I knew this only because I could feel movement, my hands were completely dead to me from lack of circulation. When he was finished, I tried to shake them to get the blood flowing again. I knew I wasn't any good to myself, or anyone else, like this. As the feeling of pins and needles attacked my hands, I began rubbing them together to speed up the process of the blood flowing back into my reawakened limbs. I looked up at Ben and smiled.

"Don't try anything stupid, Angel. I may not have killed you, yet, but that doesn't mean I would hesitate if I have to make that choice." He stood, before turning back to me.

I nodded, and started to get up. All of the blood rushed to my feet and I almost fell over. My head throbbed. My heart beat fast. Ben jumped to my side, steadied me, and then helped me walk to the small bathroom. I stopped at the door and looked at him.

"You aren't going to watch me, are you?" I asked in despair. I knew the chances of me being alone while untied were slim, but was still hopeful I could sweet talk him into letting me have a little privacy. As I looked inside of the bathroom, my hopes of jumping out of a window were squashed. "There aren't any windows in here, so it's not like I can jump out." I forced a little laugh. He looked at me for a minute, contemplating, then decided there was no harm in letting me use the restroom alone.

"Keep the door cracked. You have two minutes."

I pulled the door so it barely touched the jam, and stopped in front of the mirror. I noticed my face was covered in dried blood. I felt my head, and it had a massive knot on it. That explained the horrible pain. They really did a number on me, I thought. I could really use an ibuprofen right now. I threw water on my face, grabbed a towel and wiped dry. Staring at the reflection in the mirror, I almost laughed. Last night, I was worried about Shelly making me look like a whore. I was a mess. Shaking my head, I dried my hands and stared at the cracked out whore who stared back at me.

I sat on the toilet. There were Styrofoam cups wrapped up individually on the sink, so I filled one with water and gulped it down, choking in my haste. How was I going to get out of here? I surveyed the area again, losing all hope. There wasn't even a vent for me to sneak through. I spotted a sample size of hairspray the motel gives out, along with shampoos and soaps as a complimentary gift. I picked it up, took the cap off, and held it behind, hidden behind the cup of water still in my hand. I flushed the toilet and walked out into the room. I felt guilty for what I was about to do, but I knew no matter what Ben had planned for me, it was not going to be a happy ending.

Ben was standing by the window again, peeking through the curtains. . As I neared him, I noticed the gun tucked into the back of his pants, sticking out where his shirt had come up from him leaning over. My original plan left me. I had a new plan. I stepped closer to him, quietly. He turned to look at me. As he did, I dropped the cup of water. He looked down at the mess, I took the hairspray and started spraying him right in the face. I didn't stop until the can ran out. Both of his hands came up to his eyes as he screamed, and he turned away from me. I grabbed his gun and aimed it at him. I was shaking like a leaf, trying to not seem as nervous as I really was. I hated guns. His hand automatically went to where his gun was. Once he realized it was gone, he moaned.

"What the fuck Angel?!" He stood there wiping his eyes. "Why would you do that? I'm on your side! I'm the only reason you're even alive right now, and this is what I fucking get?" He finally got enough of the hairspray out of his eyes to glare at me. I could see the damage I had done. His eyes were horribly blood shot and red glowed all around them.

"What? You're going to shoot me now?"

"I don't want to, Ben, but damn straight I will if you make me. Don't move!" I backed toward the door slowly. "Now, you're going to tell me exactly where Shelly is."

"Yeah, right. I'm not telling you shit." He stood definitely before me. "Abe would kill us both, and I'm sorry, but you and your friend just aren't worth it to me. You won't make it out of here alive, Angel. Just give me the gun and we can talk this out." He took a small step toward me. I cocked the gun, surprising myself that I knew how to do it. He stopped dead in his tracks and put his hands up in the air.

"Fine. You want to try to fight Abe, and save your friend all by yourself? Go ahead. But don't say I didn't warn you. We aren't the only ones here, sweetheart. There are a few clients, and their men, too." He had the balls to smile at me. I almost shot him just for the look he gave me and for calling me sweetheart. What a cocky bastard. I knew, back at the club, this guy was a creep. I could tell mainly from his shirt that was too tight.

"I'd rather take my chances on dying out there," I motioned outside, "than dying in here and not doing anything at all. I'm not going to let Shelly get hurt, by you guys or anyone else." My hand shook and the gun wavered a little. Ben moved like he was going to come at me. I steadied my hand once more. "Damn it, I said don't move, Ben!"

He laughed at me, actually laughed at me. I saw the look of a crazed man in his eyes as he moved closer. He wasn't afraid of me, or the gun I held. Finally, I closed my eyes and squeezed the trigger. The sound of the gun deafened me. In mid-step, Ben went down, face first. As he lay there, I stared at the red puddle soaking into the cheap carpeting. I shook uncontrollably. What have I done? Did I seriously just shoot someone? How did it come to this?

My hearing returned, slowly, but there was a horrible ringing in my ears. The last time I heard that noise, I was 7— the day my mom died and my dad killed himself. I was frozen, taken back to the horrible day, the day my life changed forever. I swore to my grandma, on that day, all those years ago, I would never touch a gun. It was a promise I'd kept until now., and look what happened. I just shot a man. A bad man, but still a human being. Until tonight, I never believed anyone deserved to die.

I instinctively reached back and locked the door. I looked at Ben, who didn't look to be breathing. I didn't want him dead. I just wanted him to stop coming at me. Guilt grabbed my mind. As I was watching him, still waiting to see if he would breathe, someone tried the handle of the door, wiggling it. They were trying to come in. I shifted my attention to the door, away from Ben.

THUNK! THUNK! THUNK!

Somebody pounded on the door. The shot was loud. Everyone in the area would have heard it. Ben was right. Now I was going to have deal with all of their clients, their men, coming after me. I was back to square one.

# CHAPTER FOUR

THUNK! THUNK! THUNK! Again somebody beat on the door.

"Ben! What the fuck are you trying to do — bring the cops to us? You're a moron, man! You were supposed to take the bitch away from here, then take care of her — not shoot her in here in the damned motel. I can't depend on you for shit." It was Abe. I could hear the familiar snarl in his voice. The doorknob jiggled again, followed by more pounding. "Ben! Open the fucking door! Ben! Fuck!" He punched the door, hard.

My breathing sped and my heart pounded, almost making me dizzy. Now what do I do? I can't just open the door and start shooting. I need someone to tell me where Shelly was. The pounding on the door stopped and the silence scared me. I knew, any time now, Abe was going to bust the door down. I aimed the gun at the door and waited. I needed to think about how I was going to make my next move. First, figure out how to get out of this room alive, next, find Shelly, and then finally, get us both to safety.

Gunshots. Many gunshots. I couldn't even count how many there were. What was going on? Did Abe get mad and shoot

Shelly? Didn't his client like what he saw, and have everyone else shot? If any of those were true, my world would be over. Any hope would be gone.

"Please, God, let Shelly be okay. Please don't let me be too late," I prayed out loud. My head started hurting again. Or had it even stop? I didn't know, but it sure was hurting now. I felt something roll down my forehead. I reached up and wiped it off. It was blood. I must have reopened a cut during my struggle with Ben. I looked over at him and became nauseous. I walked over to the bed, grabbed a sheet, and threw it over him. I sauntered over to my spot in front of the door, and waited.

I don't know how long I stood there, with the gun pointing at the door, knowing something was bound to happen any moment now. Just as I decided I had gotten brave enough to open it, someone pounded on it again. I jumped for the second time that night. My bravery disappeared as soon as it showed its face.

"Police! Open up!" Someone yelled from outside. I didn't know the voice, but I was afraid one of Abe's men or his clients' men would be on the other side of the door. Anyone can say they are the police. Even if it was the police, did I want them to see the damage I had caused?

I was still in shock, dealing with what I did, not to mention every other event that had taken place in the past twenty-four hours. I didn't think to look out of the peep hole of the door. Instead, being the coward I am, I ran to the bathroom and locked the door. As soon as I turned the lock, there was a loud bang on the other side of the door.

I heard a lot of rustling. Someone yelled, " Clear!" There was silence. "We have a body here! Male. She's got to be here somewhere. Someone check the bathroom!"

I was terrified. They sounded like the police. If they were, would they arrest me for murder? I mean, I did kill someone.

I began to hyperventilate with the thought of going to jail. At the same time, what if it wasn't the police? They could still be lying. I looked around the bathroom again, hoping I had missed something in my haste earlier with Ben. No such luck. There was definitely no escaping this room. Contemplating my next move, there was a soft knock on the bathroom door.

"Angel? Are you in there?" Could it be? It sounded a lot like Shelly!

Was I hallucinating? She sounded very little, not like the Shelly I have known since our freshman year of high school. She had always been larger than life, had always had the voice that carried for what seems like miles. Maybe Abe got one of his other victims to come and look for me. I didn't know, but it took everything I had in me to find out.

"Shelly?" I asked in a whisper. I was afraid, but there was only one way to know.

"Angel! Yes, it's me! Are you okay? Please tell me that you're alright. I heard a shot come from this room earlier before the police showed up. Have you been shot? Open the door honey." Now that was the Shelly I knew and loved. She sounded excited and tired at the same time, but at least I knew it was her, for sure. That meant she was alright. It meant she wasn't sold to some creepy old man, and she was alive.

My hands relaxed and I dropped the gun on the floor with a loud clunk. I flinched, thinking it could go off on its own. It didn't. Instead, it laid there on the floor in front of the toilet.

I stood up and walked toward the bathroom door. As I unlocked it, I could only think about the fact that Ben's body was on the other side. I would have to face the police and the fact I was a murderer. Where was Abe and all of these other men Ben was talking about? Did they get away, or did they get arrested?

I heard Shelly's voice on the other side of the door,. A male voice replied. It was muffled so I couldn't make out what they were saying. I opened the door. Shelly ran up and threw her arms around me, making me grunt with pain.

"Angel! Oh my God, I'm so glad you're okay! Are you okay?" she asked as she looked me from head to toe. She must have noticed the blood on my face and in my hair. Her eyes widened. Tears streamed down her face as she inspected me for more injuries. She noticed the blood on my shoulders and she paled .

I looked at her just as closely, doing the same thing. I couldn't believe she was still here. She wasn't sold to some creep who would use her up and throw her away. The relief that washed over me was so intense I slid down the wall to the floor. There were officers everywhere, it seemed. I glanced over to where Ben was, and there was an officer pulling down the sheet I had covered him with. I took one look at him, and threw up what little I had in me at the time.

"I… I killed him… I'm a murderer… I killed Ben, Shelly." I wiped my mouth with the back of my hand. I glanced at Shelly and her look confused me. "Why are you looking at me like that? I'm a murderer. I took his gun and I shot him." I didn't know why I was saying this out loud when I should be trying to defend myself, pleading my case. I shouldn't have been confessing, and giving them a good reason to throw me in prison for the rest of my life.

An officer came over to me and lifted me up off of the floor. He must be strong, to lift me like I weighed nothing, I thought. I felt an immediate calm wash over me, as if my body was soaking up some of his strength.

"You shot him in self-defense, Miss Brady. He was going to kill you." Hearing that from someone else's mouth was the last straw. Everything came crashing down on me and my world went black again.

• • • • • • • •

I awakened to an annoying beeping sound and there was something on my arm, squeezing it tightly. Where am I? Am I a prisoner still? Was being rescued, and seeing Shelly, all a dream? I paniced. I opened my eyes. Relief flooded through me. I was in a hospital room. I looked to my right and spotted Shelly. She was sleeping in the chair beside my bed. I looked around the rest of the room. It was so bright that it took my eyes a few minutes to adjust.

There were two officers standing outside of the door. I took a good look again at Shelly as she slept. Other than the dark circles under her eyes, she looked unharmed. I breathed a sigh of relief. I thought about Ben. The poor guy probably didn't even know what he was getting into when he hooked up with Abe. I wondered what could make someone, who seemed so nice, get involved with someone so evil. I paused in my thoughts. Was Ben's personality just an act? I mean, the side I had seen of him when I shot him, wasn't a good one. I really didn't know him at all. I guess I'll never know the answers to those questions now, considering I took his life. I hoped his family could forgive me some day. He was, of course, someone's son.

Why am I not in a jail cell, by the way? Last night the officer said it was self-defense, which it was, but I didn't think there was a self-defense law in Ohio. I was confused. A new question came to mind. How did the police get there so fast? Did my shooting Ben make someone call them to the motel? I knew how loud it was inside the room, but was it as loud outside? I started to sit up and a sudden rush of nausea hit me. Monitor alarms sounded. I lay back down.

Shelly woke up with a start, and came to my side.

"Hey. How are you feeling Ang? I wondered if you were ever going to wake up." The concern on her face brought tears to my eyes. Here she was, almost sold as a sex slave, and she's worried sick about me.

"I'm okay. Just a little nauseous. My head is killing me. How long was I asleep?" I gazed at my hands and saw some mean looking bruises on my wrists, most likely from being tied up for so long. I lay quietly, waiting for her to say something. She stared at me for a few seconds.

"Yeah, you really have a huge knot on the top of your head." Shelly reached out and grabbed my hand to hold. "One of the guys must have hit you with something pretty hard. You were out for about 3 days after you passed out at the motel. Angel, I'm so sorry I drug you out to that stupid club! You tried so hard to get out of it." She started to cry, shaking her head. "I am never drinking again." She wiped her eyes and continued. "They put some kind of drug in my drinks at the club. That asshole, Abe, bragged about it to me. Who does that? Oh, and the club, by the way, has been shut down. The owner is under an investigation for human trafficking, too."

"What? The owner of the club is involved? Wow…" I couldn't wrap my head around everything. The club owner? I focused my attention back to Shelly. "So, Ben told me they wouldn't hurt you. Something about the client who was coming to look at you not being happy if you had any marks. Thank God for that small favor. It was the only thing that kept my hopes up you would be alright. They were going to sell you to the highest bidder, Shell." Shelly nodded slowly and began to say something when an officer tapped on the door and walked in.

"I'm sorry to interrupt, ladies, but I was wondering if I could ask Miss Brady some questions?" The officer was a tall, fit man, with black hair and icy blue eyes. He was the same officer who was at the motel when I fainted. He'd helped me off the floor before that. I remembered his strength when he picked me up.

I could get lost in those eyes, I thought. His voice is so deep, too. This man had 'sexy' written all over him… Where in the Hell did those thoughts come from? I didn't have those types of thoughts. I chastised myself for even thinking about an officer of the law like that, especially after what had transpired. I nodded to him, and he walked over to the side of the bed. I looked at Shelly who picked up her purse and smiled at me.

"I'll be back in a little bit, Angel. I need to get a cup of coffee and walk off these stiff legs." She hugged me. "I love you so much."

"Okay. I love you too, Shell," I whispered. I then turned my attention to the officer in front of me. I looked at his name tag: Officer Mancini. Donovan Mancini. Donovan… such a strong name. It fit him. But those eyes… I shook off the thoughts before they could go in that direction again. I didn't want him to think that I was laying in this hospital bed, fawning all over him.

"How can I help you, officer?" I reached for the glass of water sitting on the table beside the bed. He noticed me wince as I tried, grabbed it, and handed it to me. "Thank you," I said and sipped on what was the best tasting thing I have ever had. I tipped the cupso I could get a piece of ice to chew. This was the only thing I liked about hospitals— crushed ice.

"Miss Brady…" he began.

"Angel," I interrupted.

"Okay then, Angel." He smiled and I tried not to get lost in it. "I was wondering if you could give me your version of what happened the night you and Shelly were kidnapped. Please, try not to leave any detail out. Also, if it's okay with you, I'd like to record this conversation." His eyes searched mine, which was a little unnerving. I nodded. How was I going to be able to concentrate enough to tell him what happened when he looked at me with those eyes? However, I had somehow managed to do just that, giving him every gory detail I could remember about the most horrible night of my adult life. He jotted things down in a notepad, as well as recorded my statement. Finally, he asked me to sign the written pieces of paper.

"Can I ask you a question, now?" I asked. There was something that I was dying to know.

"Sure." He looked at me warily. I noticed he had dark circles under his eyes, just like Shelly. I wondered what had kept him from his much needed sleep.

"First, is Ben dead?" I shuddered as the memory came to me. Ben never seem like a horrible person until the end, when I saw that evil look in his eyes. I knew when I saw that, it had meant I wasn't getting out of that room alive, if it were up to him. He was like night and day. One minute he was cleaning off my face, being considerate, the next, he was going to take me completely out of the picture. I understood he wanted to take the gun away from me. What I didn't understand, was why he charged me. He would probably still be alive today if he wouldn't have done that.

"Yes, Angel. He's dead. He was dead when we got to the room." Concern shadowed his eyes as he watched my reaction to the news.

"I can't believe I killed someone," I whispered.

"As I told you when we found you, it was self-defense. It wasn't looking good for you, Angel. If they weren't going to sell you along with Shelly, they would have had to figure out another way to get rid of you. You are one lucky lady." He shifted his weight on the hospital bed.

I shook my head. "How did you guys get to the motel room so fast? It couldn't have been too long from the time I shot Ben to when you were banging on the motel door. Maybe ten minutes, at most." He contemplated my question and his answer.

"Well, we didn't just show up after that shot. We heard it, but it wasn't what brought us to the scene. Don't get me wrong— it sped up the process of our sting a bit. But in all honesty, we were already there." I looked at him questioningly. He went on. "We received some tips a while back there was human trafficking going on in the area. There have been a few missing young women and teenage girls of late . We had some information about Abraham Gunner, aka Abe, being involved. We trailed him for a while. The 'Forever It Club' and that motel were frequent stops for him. Usually the motel followed after the club, and he was never alone in those rooms. We were staking out the motel that night, trying to get more on him and his cronies. When we heard the gunshot, we jumped into action. We watched as Abe rushed out of his room to yours. When no one came to the door of your room, he went back to his room and came out with your friend, Shelly. He headed for his car. We noticed Shelly had been crying and struggling, so we stopped him. He pulled out a gun and started firing at us, using Shelly as a shield. Finally, as he was getting into his car, he let go of his hold on her. It was the window we needed to immobilize him. He took a bullet to the shoulder."

He went on to explain how Shelly ran from the car screaming about her friend, Angel, which room she was in, and she could be in serious danger. That's when they came to the door. I watched him as he told his story. So it really was the police when I heard the last knock. I guess I should have looked through the peep hole after all. Hind sight…

"Wow. So why investigate the owner of the club?" Curiosity was my middle name. I really wanted to know exactly what it was we were almost involved in. This all seemed so crazy, and hearing it actually come from a cop, made it seem real. This wasn't a bad nightmare. It was real life.

"Well, when we took Abe to the hospital to be treated for the gunshot, we questioned him and he sang like a bird. He told us who he worked for, gave a list of clients' names, everything." He smiled and shook his head.. "I can't believe our luck. Usually these type of cases are rarely solved, let alone the victims coming out of it unharmed. (bring the next paragraph up to this)

"There were twelve girls in that motel. A couple of them are still in the hospital as well, with minor injuries. Some of them are in drug recovery institutions, trying to get off of what these men had given them. They had many of them addicted to heroin."

"So, Abe is in this hospital, too?" The thought of running into him chilled me to the bone. I looked quickly around the room and started to shake. It was like I was expecting him to jump out from behind the window curtains.

"Oh, no. Of course not," he quickly replied. "He was taken to a different hospital than you. We wouldn't want to take any chance of him coming after you. Anyway, he's already been fixed up and taken to a holding cell."

I exhaled the breath I unknowingly held.

"He will be held on a slew of charges," Donovan said. He won't be getting out of prison for a very long time, if ever."

That makes me feel a lot better, I thought.

"He was going to have his friend kill me. Like, actually kill me, kill me. He said his clients wouldn't want me. I wasn't desirable enough for any of them." That made me physically shiver, and Donovan brought me a blanket and covered me. I smiled gratefully at him. "Thank you," I said. He smiled back and then looked at me seriously for a minute.

"No problem. You have been through Hell and back in the past few days," Donovan said. He stopped tucking me in, as if suddenly realizing what he was doing. He started for the door. "Well, I better get out of here and let you get some rest before your friend comes in here and yells at me." Donovan smiled sheepishly.

"I'm pretty sure I got enough rest, but you should get some yourself. You look tired, as well. Thank you for coming in, officer."

I could feel my eyes getting heavy again. He was at the door of my room, and then suddenly turned back to me.

"It's Donovan. Donovan Mancini. You should be very proud of yourself, by the way, Angel. Not too many women would have been able to handle this whole situation like you did. You thought very quickly, and it saved not only your own life, but the lives of many others. You're a very strong lady. I'll be in touch." He smiled, and was gone. My eyes closed and I was in dreamland again. The pain medicine the nurse gave me was kicking in.

# CHAPTER FIVE

I was standing in the front yard of my childhood home. I had a gun in my and I was pointing it at my dad. I was so angry, but I couldn't understand why. He looked at me and screamed, "Just do it, Angel! Shoot me!"

I fought with myself for a few minutes. Why would my dad want me to shoot him, and why was I so angry at him? He looked like he was mad at me, too. He started to charge at me. I pulled the trigger. I heard someone scream.

I woke up, realizing the scream was from me. It was another nightmare and a really bad one, at that. They usually never involve my dad. I've dreamt about my mom often, but never my dad. I barely even remember what he looked like. Sure, Grandma has a ton of pictures of him around the house, but for the longest time, I refused to look at them. It was like my young mind blocked him out. He wasn't a bad father, but I guess I have grown to live with the anger of him leaving me years ago. By his own choice. At least when my mom died, it wasn't her choice to leave me. My dad chose to end his own life. Grandma tried to explain to me he wasn't himself, that he was sick. She said he would never want to leave me if he was right in his head. The grief of losing my mom had pushed him over the edge. Even knowing this information, I didn't care. I still was upset with him..

I was shaking, and soaked with sweat. I looked at my cell phone on the nightstand. 5:30 A.M. I had to work at the diner at 9:00 A.M. However, I knew there was no way that I was going back to sleep, so I dragged myself out of bed and went to take a shower.

As I held myself away from the shower's wall and let the rushing water massage my back, my mind wandered. It had been 2 weeks since the incident with the Abe and Ben, the human traffickers. The victim's advocate the state had appointed me said the nightmares would eventually go away with therapy. It was extremely frustrating to see a therapist while working on the same degree used to help others in my situation. How was I supposed to help others when I couldn't even help myself?

One session so far and the therapist concluded I suffered from Post-Traumatic Stress Disorder. I knew what it was; I remembered studying about it in my Abnormal Psychology class. He claimed it could take months, or years even, before I would be able to sleep another complete night through. Apparently, the human brain can only handle so much stress before it affects the your way when both awake and asleep.

Shelly seemed to be handling things okay, though I haven't seen her as much as I did before all of this went down. She still blames herself for what had happened that night, even with me telling her all of the time that it wasn't her fault. She had no way of knowing what was going to happen, and she was in just as much danger as I was, if not more. However, no matter how many times I tried to explain that to her, she wasn't hearing any of it.

I stretched my head back and allowed the waters to race through my locks then down my body.

Officer Mancini — Donovan the Cop, as I had secretly named

him — called when I was released from the hospital to see how I was doing at home. He also called a couple of more times after that. My heart always did a little flip when I heard his voice on the phone. I would tell him I was fine. If he knew any better, he didn't say so, though I'm pretty sure he did. I was lying to myself, along with everyone else, when I said that. I was afraid to be home all alone. I think too much. This is the one time I wished I had a roommate. It gets too quiet in an empty apartment. I had several inner demons who wanted to be heard when I was alone.

Donovan told me, at the end of every conversation, he would call me again to check on me soon. I couldn't wait for that phone call. His voice seemed to calm me. Feeling comfort in that thought, I smiled, turned off the water and stepped out of the shower.

Pouring the coffee for my drive to work, my cell phone rang. I didn't recognize the number, so I ignored it. That's a bad habit of mine. If it is important, they'll leave a message, right? I went back to my task of grabbing vanilla caramel creamer and a packet of hot chocolate from the cupboard. I added a little of each to my cup. Shelly always makes fun of how I prepare my coffee. She couldn't understand why I added the hot chocolate. I explained if I could taste the coffee itself, then I didn't want it. I only drank coffee to give me an extra push in the morning, and to warm me in the winter.

My phone beeped. Voicemail. I guess it was an important phone call, after all. I topped off my cup, put the lid on, grabbed my phone, purse, and rushed out of the door to my car. I started the car, pushed the voicemail icon on my phone, and headed to work with my phone precariously wedged between my shoulder and ear.

"Miss Brady? Angel?... Umm... This is Donovan Mancini... from the police department. Can you please call me as soon as you get this? It is extremely important ." I heard panic in his voice and was immediately afraid. . I hurriedly worked the missed call icon and pushed send. It rang once..

"Angel?" Donovan asked quickly.

"Yes, Donovan. What's up? I'm heading to work right now." I turned into the parking lot of the diner.

"I am on my way. I'll meet you there." He hung up.

I sat there and stared at my phone in confusion and frustration. Did he just hang up on me? I hated when people did that! I shook my head and opened the door to walk into work.

"I wonder what was so important he couldn't tell me over the phone?" I mumbled and put on my apron.

"What was that, sweetie?" Suzy, the manager, asked me as she walked out of the kitchen. Her hands were full of plates, waiting to be stocked on the counter.

"Oh, I was just talking to myself, Suzy. Officer Mancini, the police officer I told you about, just called me. I guess he is meeting me here. I'm not sure what is going on, or what is so important." I started to put the pop machine together.

My grandma didn't want me to go back to work so soon, but I was going crazy. . I had to do something and sitting alone in my apartment wasn't it. I was all caught up on my school work. The diner was all I had left. Shelly hadn't answered my phone calls for a couple of days, so I didn't even have anyone to hang out with. I figured I may as well make some money.

"Hmm... that is a bit odd," Suzy said. I loved Suzy. She was in her mid-sixties, but still spunky. She and I hit it off right away. She kind of filled a void in my life, like a motherly figure. In the 4 years I had worked at the diner, she had become one of my dearest friends.

I was filling ice bins up when the door chimed, letting me know someone had walked in. I began to say we weren't open yet, but then my eyes landed on Donovan. My heart did that little flip again as our eyes met. Why did that keep happening? Maybe it was that hero complex I had learned about in class. Women often develop crushes on the men they felt had saved their lives. Yeah, right. I was too old for crushes. I shook off the feelings he ignited in me, and met him in the dining room. He looked terrified, but relieved at the same time. He kept glancing around the diner, out the windows, and then back at me. He acted like the boogeyman was about to jump out. He finally sat down at a table and sighed.

"We have to go somewhere, Angel. We have to get you out of here. You aren't safe." His eyes were huge, almost like they would bulge out anytime now.

"What are you talking about, Donovan? You aren't making any sense, and you're scaring me." I sat down across from him and stared, waiting. He looked up at me and then back down at his pants as he was picking off a piece of imaginary lint.

"I don't know how to tell you this, but…" He looked straight into my eyes, and then stood abruptly. "You're in serious danger, Angel. Abe escaped from the officers during his transport from court back to jail." He waited until it all sank in before he began again. "We have to get you somewhere away from here — somewhere safe. Do you have somewhere you can stay for a little while?"

I felt my blood run cold, my heart started pounding, and I became nauseous. Abe escaped? How does that even happen these days? What am I going to do? Think, Angel, think.

"The only places that I could go would be Shelly's or my grandmother's. I refuse to go there and put either of them in danger. There is nowhere else. I have no other family, nor any real friends that I would put this on." I was beginning to feel very alone again.

"Shelly has been informed and is going to her mother's in

Florida. She said she has been trying to call you for an hour now." He searched my eyes . I wondered if he could see the pure fear in them. I didn't think I could hide it from him. He seemed to see right through my tough façade. "It'll be okay, Angel, we will figure something out. Until then, you're stuck with me. I'm not going to leave you alone." I nodded and slowly stood up. I had to force my legs to move.

"What are you doing?" he asked, watching me.

"I have to get this place ready to be open in 15 minutes," I said as I started setting the tables up with salt and pepper shakers. I could feel his eyes follow my every move. I looked back at him, and his eyes were wide with so much astonishment, I almost had to laugh. "The diner doesn't close just because I may or may not have some sort of drama in my life." Just then, Suzy decided to make an appearance.

"Well, who is this handsome devil?" she asked as she batted her eyelashes and smiled at Donovan. I giggled to myself at her attempt to flirt with him. She was so cute.

"This is Officer Donovan Mancini. Donovan, this is my boss, Suzy." They shook hands and I could see the amusement on Donovan's face.

"Nice to meet you, Suzy. I wish it were on better terms, but I'm afraid I had to deliver bad news to Angel this morning." He looked over her shoulder at me and a small smile lit his face. That warmed me up a little and settled my stomach. Suzy turned around and walked up to me.

"What's going on honey?" She put her arm around my waist. There was no way to express how much comfort I got from that one small move.

I told her what had happened and watched the color drain from her face. She turned serious, clicking her tongue and shaking her head.

"Well, what are you going to do? You need to take a vacation with that hunk of a man over there," she whispered. I felt the blush come over me and looked back at Donovan. Wouldn't that be nice? I thought.

"He's just here to tell me about that piece of shit escaping, and to protect me until we can figure out what to do next, Suzy. It's not like what you think." She opened her mouth to say something else, but stopped . She mumbled unintelligible words and hustled back into the kitchen. I turned around and noticed Donovan was standing much closer now. That must have been what had shut her up.

"She seems very sweet and protective over you." He watched me work. Something about him watching my every move had butterflies going crazy in my stomach. It was as if I could feel his eyes burning into my skin. It was probably my nerves, I thought to myself.

"Yes, she is kind of like a mother hen," I went to turn the open sign around. I turned back to him. "We are officially open, so I'll apologize now for when I get too busy to talk."

"It's not a problem. I'll just make myself useful. I was a mean bus boy back in the day." He rolled up his sleeves. I laughed and went to greet the first table of customers who walked in.

The breakfast and lunch hours were actually busier than normal, which I accepted gratefully. Not only because of the money in tips I was making, but it took my mind off of my current situation for a little while. It also helped keep the butterflies in my stomach in check, knowing Donovan was right there with me. He was really a bigger help than I thought he would be. He was right, he made a great bus boy.

As my shift was ending, I realized I was pretty wiped out. I was thankful to see Molly, the next shift's server, walk in the door. She looked at Donovan, and smiled. That's when I first noticed I didn't exist when Donovan was around. Women were drawn in by him. When I looked at him, I noticed he was watching me. He didn't even look at Molly. I felt my cheeks grow warm with the attention.

Suzy told me to take off of work until Abe was caught and safely behind bars again. I tried to argue but she gave me the look that told me there was no use. As Donovan and I walked out of the building, I thanked him for helping me. I tried to give him some money, but he looked at me like I was crazy.

"I don't want your money, Angel. It was actually pretty fun. A nice change of scenery. For once, I didn't feel like there was a huge chance of me losing my life," he laughed. "Except for when that one lady didn't get her extra whipped cream on her pie. She was pretty angry..." We both laughed. As we neared my car, he stopped walking and grabbed my hand. A jolt went up my arm and made me jump.

"I'm going to follow you home so you can gather some of your things, then we need to think of a plan. You should probably call your family and tell them what's going on. You can't stay at your place. You understand that, don't you?" He was very serious. .

"Yes, I understand. Like I said earlier, my grandma is the only family I have left. I have no idea where to go, though. I mean, maybe I should take the vacation Suzy was talking about." I half joked. "Seriously, though, what do you think I should do?"

"Let me make a few calls and see what I can get figured out." He closed my car door and ran over to his car.

On the way back to my apartment, the reality of what kind of danger I was in hit me. I felt my car closing in on me, so I rolled my windows down. I felt something wet on my cheek, and realized I was crying. I hated this feeling of helplessness. I had always prided myself as being a strong, independent woman.

In high school, I quickly earned a reputation of being a little hot headed. I guess what they say about redheads is true. Back then, however, I didn't know how to control the anger I was feeling. I took it out on the other poor students, who were at the same awkward stage in their lives. I grew out of that erratic behavior by my junior year of high school and spent the next 2 years apologizing to anyone I may have hurt.

I pulled into the parking lot of my apartment complex, and looked in my rearview mirror to make sure Donovan was still behind me. He, of course, was right on my tail. I smiled, thinking about how safe I felt in his presence. At first I thought that feeling was only because he was a police officer, but then when he was helping us at the diner, I noticed there was something else about him. So he says I'm stuck with him. Well, I guess I can't think of anyone else I would rather be stuck with. At least he was nice on the eyes.

"Stop it, Angel. You can't be thinking about a cop like that," I chastised as I got out of my car. Donovan was beside me before I could even close the door.

"So I talked to my Chief, and he has a place I think would be perfect for us to stay at until that creep is caught. It is kind of a distant trip, though," he said as he followed me to my apartment door. I stopped walking.

"Us?" There goes my heart again, thumping away. I'm not sure what this guy had over me, but it needed to go away, like, yesterday.

"Well… yeah… I thought about it and I just don't think I can trust anyone else to keep as good of an eye on you as I can. Plus, I have some vacation time that has been building up for a few years now." He winked and sat at the kitchen table, waiting for my answer. "So… What do you say? Will ya have me, Miss Angel?" he asked in a silly Southern draw, which made me giggle.

I thought about it for a second, and he was right. I'm pretty sure I wouldn't feel as comfortable with anyone else as I am with

Donovan. After these past few weeks, I felt I was able to get to know him. The thought of staying somewhere with a complete stranger did not sound as good.

"Okay. I mean, as long as you don't mind playing babysitter for a little while. I can't imagine having to spend my hard earned vacation with some girl who needs to be looked after." My body, being the betrayer it is, buzzed with the thought of being alone somewhere, with him. "Where are 'we' going, anyway?" I hoped for somewhere warm, with a beach… As if reading my mind, the most perfect words came out of his mouth next.

"The Chief has a condo on an island in St. Augustine, Florida. I think it'd be perfect considering your friend is down there, too." I could have hugged him right then and there. I almost did until I realized that wouldn't be very professional of me.

I remembered he said earlier Shelly had tried calling me. I fished my cell out of my purse and noticed I had 12 missed calls plus 4 voicemails. All but one of those calls were from Shelly. The other was my grandma. The voicemails from Shelly grew increasingly panicked. I decided I needed to call both her and my grandma. Grandma was first. She picked up on the first ring.

"Hey sweetheart! How are you? How was work?" She was always so full of joy and questions. I smiled.

"Well Grandma, work was great, but I have some news. I have to go away for a little while. Are you sitting down?"

"I can be…" I listened to her suffle to a chair. "Yes, now I am. What's going on honey?" It saddened me to hear the concern in her voice and knowing it was there because of me. Again. After everything she has done for me, and I seemed to constantly be repaying her with stress and worry.

"Well, the man who hurt me and Shelly escaped from jail earlier today. I'm not safe, Grandma. Officer Mancini is here with me, and he wants me to go to Florida until the man is caught."

She was quiet for so long, I thought my phone had dropped the call. Then I heard her sniffle, and my heart broke a little bit more.

"Oh Angel, I'm sorry baby. You do what the police think is best for you. This Officer Mancini, what do you know about him? He seems like he is a good man and will take good care of you, but... as a matter of fact..." Grandma's voice lowered and sounded very demanding. "Why don't you put him on the phone really quick?" I debated for a few seconds as to whether or not I wanted to do what my grandma asked. Finally, I decided that there couldn't be much harm in it. I looked at Donovan and then handed him the phone. He looked confused, but took it and put it to his ear.

"Hello? Yes, hello Mrs. Brady.... Uh huh... Yes, ma'am... I will be with her... I won't...I will do everything in my power to make sure she is safe at all times. Alright, ma'am. You don't have to thank me... Okay... Bye now." He handed me the phone back. "She said she loves you and you are to call her when we get to Florida." He chuckled a little bit. I could almost feel the rumble in his chest as he did. It was a nice sound.

"She's something else," I laughed, "but she raised me all by herself, when I had no one else." My voice was full of pride. I had nothing negative to say about my grandma. She was the strongest woman I have ever known.

"Alright, I have to call Shelly now before she has a coronary." I dialed her number. She answered on the first ring as well. For once, when I called, she answered.

"Girl, I swear, if you ever scare me like that again, I'm going to kick your ass!" She was screaming at me, voice full of panic.

"Jeez, I love you too, Shell," I gritted out. She must not have remembered I had been trying to get a hold of her for the past couple of days without any return phone calls. Not even a text message. I looked down at my fingernails. Wow, they needed cut.

"I'm sorry, but when the police station called to tell me about Abe's escape, and then you didn't answer, I was seriously freaking out. I couldn't find you, and the police couldn't tell me anything. I didn't know you went back to work already." The words tumbled out all in one rush of breath.

"You would have known if you ever called me back, Miss Thing," I said.

"I know. Look Ang, I don't want to argue. What are you going to do? Why don't come to my parents' place with me, in Miami? We have plenty of room."

"Actually, Officer Donovan and I are going to St. Augustine." I looked over at him and winked, knowing full well what was going through Shelly's head right now.I was going to enjoy this a little bit.

"Officer who? Is that the same one who came to the hospital?"

"One and the same."

"Oh… Wait… Oh!! Are you sleeping with him?" I could hear the amusement in her voice, mixed with a little bit of shock. I guess the thought of me having sex was unheard of these days.

"What? No! He's just going with me for protection, Shell." I glanced at Donovan, who was now watching me with his full attention, a huge grin on his face. He knew exactly which direction this conversation had went. I felt my face heat up and looked away.

"Ah, I see… I guess that makes sense, but just so you know, he didn't ask me to run away with him and I would have. He's sexy as hell," she said. She's lucky I didn't have her on speaker phone. She would have been all kinds of embarrassed. I almost wanted to do it, just to get her back. "Call me when you get there. I love you, Angel." She was gone. What was it with everyone hanging up on me these days? I turned my attention back to Donovan.

"So, when do we leave?" I asked.

"As soon as you're ready. Our plane leaves in an hour and a

half," he said as he glanced at his watch. My eyes grew wide and I ran off to my room to start packing. An hour and a half? How was I going to get everything in order in that time?

I called my neighbor, and asked if she could pick up my mail while I was gone. She wanted to know what was going on. I told her I would explain more when I got back from Florida. First, I didn't really have the time to explain, and second, she was a very nosy lady, not to mention, a gossip. The entire apartment complex would know before I even left if I told her. I hung up quickly and went back to my task at hand.

I think I grabbed every item of clothing I had and was careful to remember to bring my bathing suit. It was mid-July, so I knew I would want it. Twenty minutes later, I was out the door, pulling my suitcase behind me and a carry-on over my shoulder.

We walked down the apartment complex hallway. "I'm ready. I didn't know what to pack since I don't know how long we will be there," I explained.

He laughed

"You don't have to explain anything to me. Most women would have three times that amount for a trip." He took the suitcase out of my hand.

I was heading to Florida, with beaches and the ocean sounds, and Donovan...

# CHAPTER SIX

A s we stepped out of the airport, out into the Florida air, it was like being hit by a brick wall. It was hard to breathe. The humidity was high and it had to be at least 100 degrees out. I reached back and pulled my hair into a pony tail as I followed Donovan. He waved to who I assumed was the driver to our next destination. I looked in the direction of where he was waving and gasped. We were riding in a limo? Interesting, but I wasn't complaining.

The driver took our bags and put them in the trunk. He then opened the back door. I slid in and looked around. This wasn't just any limo. I glanced at Donovan, confused. He chuckled and the opened a hidden door I hadn't noticed when we got in. I watched as he pulled out a bottle of champagne and two long stemmed glasses. He made something as simple as pouring champagne seem so sensual. He filled them both and handed one to me.

"The Chief has expensive taste. To a well-deserved vacation," he said and winked at me. I took a sip and smiled back. I was nervous now that we were alone in the back of this fancy car. I looked away, down to my glass, only to find I had emptied it already. He filled it and I had to force myself from drinking it down again.

I was beginning to think the air conditioning in the car wasn't working, as I was feeling warm. It was probably because of the champagne. I didn't normally drink champagne and the two glasses were already affecting me. I had a serious buzz. Maybe it was from the plane ride. Donovan picked up the bottle with an amused look on his face and I shook my head. I had had enough. Any more and I would be making bad decisions.

"So, how far away is the condo from here?" I asked, trying to start up a conversation before the nervous energy drove me insane. I looked out of the car window with an attempt to get my mind right.

"Only about fifteen minutes," he answered.

Thank you! I thought to myself as I nodded. Any longer in this vehicle alone with him and I'd probably make a fool out of myself by doing, or saying, something stupid. How was I going to stay in the same place alone with him for any long period of time?

It wasn't long and we were pulling up in front of what looked like a mansion. It had to be at least three stories tall with the most beautiful white pillars in the front. The yard was in pristine condition with gardeners working on it. We got out of the car and I was in total shock. This place is amazing, I thought.

"Are you kidding me? This is a condo?" I said. It took everything I had not to jump for joy when I noticed the ocean out back. I was definitely going to enjoy this place. We walked up the stairs of the porch.

We were greeted at the door by Ellen, as she introduced herself, the housekeeper. She would be staying with us during our visit here. A housekeeper? I have never been spoiled like this. I didn't particularly like the idea of having someone wait on me, hand and foot but I was willing to allow it. She led us to our rooms and I gasped again when I looked at mine. Ellen smiled at the little squeak that came out of my mouth.

"I'll let you get settled in. Just let me know if you need anything, Miss Brady," she said and let herself out.

I lifted my suitcase onto the bed and started to unpack. I looked out of my window at the ocean that spread out as far as I could see. It was so beautiful, with its white sand and waves. Once I had put everything away, I went to the bathroom. As soon as I saw the huge Jacuzzi garden bathtub, I decided a bath was definitely the first thing on my "to do " list. My muscles were so tense, I assumed, from stress and the busy work day. I turned on the faucets and added some of the rose smelling salts. I undressed and put on my robe, then went into my room to pick out something else to wear. I chose the yellow sundress I had brought.

As I was heading back into the bathroom, there a soft knock on the door. I tied my robe and went to see who it was, thinking maybe the housekeeper forgot to tell me something. I was wrong. Donovan stood there, speechless. He just stared at me. I started to blush as I could feel his eyes traveling all over me.

"Um… Hey…" He cleared his throat and snapped out of it, then looked me in the eyes. "I was wondering if you wanted to go out for a bite to eat tonight, or if you wanted to stay in for dinner?"

"Oh! Well, I thought I would take a bath and then maybe go for a walk on the beach. My brain hasn't made it to dinner yet. There is just so much going on here." I laughed nervously and motioned at the house to show what I meant. The way he was looking at me had my heart fluttering, my mind racing, and I was rambling. This was new to me. I never rambled. I've always had my head on straight.

"Okay," he said as he looked me up and down, once more, appreciatively. "I'll let you get back to your bath. I'll get out of this uniform, then we can go for that walk." He started to amble away, but I wasn't quite ready to see him go just yet.

"Thank you, Donovan. For everything," I said. He turned around to look at me. "I honestly don't know what I would do without you right now. I know this is a scary situation, but I feel very at ease since you are here with me." I shyly smiled and closed the door before he could say anything. Besides, there was a massive bathtub calling out to my aching muscles.

I walked to the bathroom and took off my robe. I slowly sunk down into the perfect hot water., My mind drifted before I found myself thinking about the events of the day. Abe was out, running loose, and here I was, kind of a prisoner once again. That thought brought on a familiar chill. I was still trying to figure out how that happened. I didn't even think it was possible for inmates to escape from officers or jail these days. I guess I was wrong. I would have to ask Donovan about that later.

My mind wandered back to Donovan, with his tall, dark and handsome features. I wondered what he looked like out of his uniform. I imagined him in a pair of shorts, without a shirt on, all of those rippling muscles... I sighed and smiled at the picture produced, then sunk lower into the hot water.

I soaked for about an hour, the water cooled off, so I grudgingly stood up, turned the shower on, washed and rinsed my hair before stepping out to dry off. I brushed my hair and pulled my dress over my head. I looked in the mirror, decided to put my hair in a messy bun and threw on some eyeliner and mascara. I sprayed a little perfume on and started toward the door to search for Donovan.

He was waiting for me in the kitchen, sitting at the table, typing on his laptop. Since he was busy, I took the opportunity to watch him. He really was a beautiful man. He had a chiseled face, with a straight nose, and perfectly kissable lips. The baby blue t-shirt he was wearing fit him perfectly so I could see every muscle as he moved. He had to work out on a regular basis in order to have a body like that. The khaki shorts revealed well-toned legs — and a tan.

He glanced in my direction, catching me staring. The shirt he was wearing made his blue eyes stand out even more, if that was possible. I smiled guiltily, busted. He smiled back and closed his laptop.

"I thought you were supposed to be on vacation. What are you doing? Bringing work with you?" I teased.

"Actually, if you must know, I was looking up things to do in St. Augustine." he He stood up, and winked at me. Donovan slid a glass door open, waved his hand toward the outside and I laughed as we started out toward the beach.

As we walked, we got to know each other a little bit. I told him about my grandma, and my mom. I didn't really want to tell him everything about my dad, but I did talk a little bit about him. . I learned Donovan was thirty, divorced, with no children. He had a dog named Panchowho recently had to be put down for a brain tumor. That made me sad. I loved dogs. If I didn't live in an apartment, I would have one . However, I didn't feel it would be fair t — not having room to run around. Donovan and his parents were from San Antonio, Texas. He was an only child, like myself, and his parents were both deceased, also like me. We had a bit in common.

"So, what made you decide to become a cop?" I watched the water rush over my feet. It tickled.

"Well…" He looked thoughtful for a few seconds, as if he was deciding on whether or not to tell me. He stopped and turned toward me. "My father was a bad guy, Angel. Not just a little bad, but really bad. He was a drug lord." He watched me to see if I would react negatively to that information, which of course, I didn't. He continued.

"Anyway, he ended up making a lot of people very angry, like, big named people. One day, when I was 16, I came home from school to find him and my mom, dead. They were tied to chairs, sitting back to back. They had both been shot in the head. There was a note painted on the wall above them saying, 'You fucked with the wrong gang this time'. Anyway, I decided right then that, one, I wouldn't ever be like my dad, and two, I would be the one who arrested scumbags like people who killed my parents." He looked like he was very far away in his memory. He looked at me and I could see the sadness in his eyes. I felt his pain, losing both parents at once. I took a hold of his hand and pulled him to walk with me again.

"I didn't mean to bring up such painful memories for you, Donovan. I'm sorry," I whispered. He squeezed my hand. I looked at him. He smiled to let me know it was okay.

"It was a long time ago. I've had plenty of time to deal with the loss, the anger. You know, come to think of it, I have only told a couple of people about that." He stopped walking and pulled me closer to him. "I feel like I could tell you anything... Wait... Is that creepy?"

Well, there goes my heart again and of course, the butterflies in my stomach, I thought. There was definitely something about this guy, other than his good looks and amazing body. He was genuine.

"Not creepy at all," I said as I smiled at him. "I'm glad you feel you can talk to me. It is easy for me to talk to you, too." That made him smile which made me want to melt into a puddle, right therein the sand.

"I look forward to getting to know you better, even if these circumstances suck." Even as Donovan said it, I shuddered. He looked at me apologetically. "I'm sorry this is happening to you, Angel. This should all be over for you, not beginning all over again." His voice was laden thick with regret. Donovan laced his fingers with mine and squeezed.

"It's not your fault, Donovan. Plus, look at us. We get to have a free vacation because of it." I tried to lighten the mood eventhough I knew that this was, indeed, a scary situation. If Abe found me, he'd make sure he finished what his friend couldn't. I would be a goner. The thought terrified me. I could only imagine what he had going on in that dark mind of his. Before my imagination could go into overdrive, and cause me to have a panic attack, I looked into Donovan's eyes. Much better.

"Let's go find something to eat. I'm starving and was thinking we could stay in tonight. I'll let you show me the town tomorrow." I attempted to change the subject. He smiled and nodded. We turned around to start the trek back to the condo. As we neared the big house, I noticed something shiny in the sand.

"What do you think that is?" I asked Donovan. His eyes followed to where I was pointing my finger.

"Not sure. Let me go see." He let go of my hand and ran over to the object. I immediately missed his presence next to me. I watched him kneel down, pick it up, and run back toward me. He looked like a little boy, extremely excited to show me the prize. When he reached me, he held out his hand and I squealed with delight. It was a diamond studded earring — and it was at least 3 carats big.

"Wow! I bet someone is very upset they lost that. " I laughed. "We should find the police station tomorrow while we are out and turn it in."

He looked at me with admiration in his eyes and then nodded. He grabbed my hand and we continued to walk to the condo. I was going to enjoy this time with Donovan, even if it was only for a few days. He made me feel comfortable and safe. He also made me feel pretty, which is way more than I could say about the others I had dated in the past. I was definitely not used to someone appreciating my presence. My past experiences were normally a "wham, bam, thank you ma'am" sort of thing. Not with Donovan, though. This was really a nice contrast.

Dinner was delicious. We had sent the housekeeper home before we went for our walk on the beach, so Donovan decided he would show me his culinary skills. I was not disappointed at all. He made grilled salmon, scalloped potatoes, and topped the whole dinner off with the most amazing cheesecake I had ever tasted. He admitted to finding the cheesecake in the freezer earlier in the day. I didn't care, of course, as it was still great.

After dinner, we went our separate ways. I went to my room so I could check my schooling online to be sure I wasn't missing anything. Donovan wanted to check in with his chief; he would be busy as well. I closed down the school's website on my phone and glanced at the time. It was 1:30AM. Wow! It's late, I thought. I crawled into the welcoming bed. That was the last thing I thought about before my eyes slammed shut.

# CHAPTER SEVEN

I was in my apartment, wondering how I had gotten there. As I looked around, everything seemed off. My couch didn't look the same, my blinds were the wrong color, and many other things just didn't fit. I was definitely at my place. Somehow I knew that much. I looked around again. What happened to Donovan? Where did he go?

I saw him. He was lying on the floor, blood oozing from his head. I ran over to him and looked around frantically for something to stop the bleeding. The closest room was the kitchen. I knew I had towels in there. I looked at Donovan again, and he didn't seem to be breathing. I reached down to his neck to check for a pulse. It was very faint, but it was there. I was sure of it. I stood quickly.

As I ran to the kitchen, someone grabbed me around the waist. I screamed but nothing came out. I was thrown onto the couch. I saw who was roughing me up. My heart dropped with dread. Abe stood glowering above me. He had a gun pointed at my head. The edges of his lips curled in a wicked smile. His arm slowly swung around and pointed at Donovan.

"NO!!" I yelled. He didn't even flinch. I grabbed the gun.

Abe wasn't there. It was me — holding the gun. Donovan was no longer on the floor — it was Ben. He slowly stood, blood covering him from head to toe. He stood, jumped on me, and tackled me to the ground with nonhuman speed. He held me on the floor, bleeding everywhere on me. I screamed again. This time, my voice filled the room.

"Angel! Angel! Wake up!" Donovan shook my shoulder. "You're having a bad dream. Wake up." I sat, sure my heart was going to jump out of my chest. I couldn't breathe. I slowly focused on my surroundings, calming myself down, and realized I was in my room at the condo. I wasn't in my apartment. I scanned the room. There was no Abe, and no Ben. I breathed slowly. Donovan sat beside me, terrified. He was not bleeding. That fact calmed me even more. It had been a dream. A nightmare, and one of the worst ones I could ever remember having.

"Are you okay? You were screaming bloody murder. I thought someone was trying to kill you." He gently stroked my hair, pushing it behind my ears so he could see my face.

"It was a horrible nightmare. I've been having them since the kidnapping, literally, every single night." I shivered. "This one was really bad." I looked down at my shirt which was soaked in sweat.

"Want to talk about it?" Donovan held my shoulders in his strong hands, his thumbs softly massaging me. "Sometimes, if you talk about your nightmare, you won't have the same one again. I don't know how much truth there is to that, but, it couldn't hurt, right?" Once he was sure I was physically alright, he went into the bathroom and filled a cup of water. He handed it to me as he sat back down beside me.

"Thank you," I said as I took a drink. "I don't know if I'm ready to go into details, but this one was especially bad." I shuddered at the memory. The vision of Donovan lying on the floor, bleeding to death from a head wound, frightened me more than any other part of the dream. I stood, walked over to the dresser, and grabbed another tank top to change into. I strode toward the bathroom.

"Okay," Donovan said. "I'm here if you change your mind. I won't push it." He stalled for a few seconds, obviously trying to decide what he should do. " Guess I should let you get some rest..."

I stopped in my tracks, and turned back to him.

"Don't go, Donovan, please. Just stay with me for a little bit," I begged. I could not bear to be alone right now. There was no way I was going back to sleep, not after that dream. I changed my shirt quickly, and hustled back to the bed.

"Okay, no problem, honey. I will stay as long as you need me to," he soothed and settled back down on the bed beside me. It was thenI noticed he only had on a pair boxers. Well, this is convenient, I thought with a small smile. It makes it a lot easier to check him out when he's half naked in front of me. He had a tattoo of angel wings going from one shoulder to the other and half way down his back. It just made him that much more perfect. I loved tattoos.

I scooted over, pulled the sheets back, and motioned for him to lie down beside me. He hesitated only for a breath, and then lay down. He reached for my hand and pulled me into his arms. As he wrapped them around me, I lay my head on his chest. There was no place I would rather be, than where I was at that moment, listening to his steady heartbeat. He reached up and ran his hand through my hair, pushing it away from my face. His other hand trailed his fingers up and down my back. Even as the goose bumps were raised on my skin, the motion calmed me immensely.

"Thank you, for staying with me. I knew that there was no way I could calm myself alone," I murmured into his chest. I trailed my finger over it as I spoke, grazing a nipple. He groaned and grabbed my hand to hold it still. My head vibrated with the sound.

"You don't have to thank me, Angel. I'm glad I can help, in any way." He's such a gentleman, I thought. For once, I kind of wished he wasn't. Not that I was well-experienced in the area of sex. The two guys I had been with prior were in such a hurry, it was over before it began. I tried to clear the thoughts of Donovan doing immoral things to me. It didn't work. The fact he was in my bed, almost naked, and holding me, didn't help the direction of my thoughts at all.

As if he could read my mind, he turned onto his side, and positioned me to where my back was to his front. He threw his arm around my waist and pulled me closer. We fit perfectly together, like two spoons. I couldn't help but wiggle my butt a little bit closer. I smiled mischievously as his grip tightened around my belly, his erection evident. I closed my eyes and attempted to go back to sleep. I really did try, I swear.

We lay there for quite a while, no sleep in sight. I sighed and turned onto my back. Donovan was awake. He propped up on his elbow and looked down at me.

"Sleep is evading you, too, huh?" he murmured with a deep voice in my ear, which did crazy things to my insides. I looked at him and nodded.

"I tried. I mean, I'm really comfortable, but it just won't come to me." That statement made him laugh, and I could see in the moonlight his eyes shining with amusement at my choice of words. It hit me, what I had said.

"That's not what I meant!" I giggled as I lightly smacked his chest. He laughed. All amusement left his eyes. Something completely different replaced his look.

I bit my lip, wondering what he was thinking. I didn't have to wonder for very long. He leaned in and lightly touched his lips to mine. My body responded immediately and I turned onto my side to face him. I wrapped my arms around his neck and rolled back onto my back, pulling him with me. He took the kiss deeper. I kissed him back with everything I had, our tongues dancing. I felt like I couldn't get close enough to him, as if he would disappear if I let go. When he lifted his head, we were both breathless.

"I'm sorry. I shouldn't have done that. You're at a venerable point in your life and I'm taking advantage. I can't seem to think straight when you are near me," he whispered and started to pull away. I ran my hands through his hair and he closed his eyes. I pulled him down to me and kissed him with desperation. I couldn't let him think this was wrong when I have never felt something more right in my life. This time, when the kiss broke, he looked me in the eyes I'll swear he could see into my soul. He had his hand on my waist and slowly brought it up so it rested just below my breast. His thumb skimmed my nipple and it hardened.

He pulled me under him and I welcomed him readily. He started to kiss my neck, leaving a trail of kisses down further, and further yet, until I thought I would explode with need. He reached the bottom of my tank top and pulled it up and over my head. He stared momentarily at me in the moonlight.

"Are you sure?" he asked. Once again, the gentleman. I wasn't allowing it this time. I didn't want the gentleman Donovan could be. Not now, anyway. He could be that man again tomorrow.

"I have never been more sure about anything in my life." I pulled him to me once again, thinking about how sweet he was to worry about what I wanted. Right now, I wanted him, inside of me. He gazed at me for a few seconds, as if he was appreciating a painting. I started to feel self-conscious.

"You are so beautiful, Angel. I could look at you all night long." His strong hand slid my panties down my legs. I blushed, and shook my head.

"No, you can't. I don't think my body, or my heart could take it if you stopped and stared right now."

He chuckled, but he didn't stop. My heart would go on to beat another day, and my body would spontaneously combust.

Before tonight, I hadn't had anyone make love to me before. It was only sex. Donovan took his time with me, cherishing my body, with both his hands, and his mouth. I have never had someone kiss me "there" before. When he did, I almost climbed the walls. I decided I must let him do that more often. I also thought it would only be fair I return the favor. I knelt in front of him. He watched my every move. I must have been doing something right. He stopped me abruptly and brought me back up to him. He lay me down on the bed, and didn't waste time before entering me. I was surprised with the feeling of fullness that had provided. He made love to me that night. He made me feel beautiful. He made me feel safe. Most importantly, he made feel loved. I felt like a Goddess.

I knew he loved my body, I didn't know how he felt about me as a person. I only knew one thing for certain, and that was how I had felt about him. I didn't know it was possible to feel this way about someone I had only met a few weeks ago.

Donovan wasn't finished after that first time. He decided my body needed cherished two more times that night. I had no desire to argue with him, either. After making love all night long, we both finally fell into a deep, fulfilling, and much needed, slumber. I fell asleep, vaguely thinking about the fact we hadn't used any protection.

# CHAPTER EIGHT

The next morning, I woke up in Donovan's arms. It was as if we didn't move once we finally fell asleep. I had to use the bathroom, but I didn't want to disturb his sleep. I slowly untangled my legs from his and tried to get out of the bed, attempting to be as quiet as possible. It didn't work.

"Good morning, gorgeous," he said. He yawned and stretched his body out on the bed.

"Good morning," I smiled and threw on the robe hanging on the footboard of the bed. I rushed into the bathroom and closed the door. Did I seriously do all of that last night? What ever happened to the Angel who never took chances, or did something on a whim? I looked at my reflection in the mirror and the woman looking back at me was smiling. At that moment, I didn't care where that Angel had gone. She could stay lost as far as I was concerned. Last night was amazing.

I brushed my teeth and realized one very important fact. I had actually slept the whole night through without waking up. I didn't have another nightmare after Donovan and I fell asleep. That was a miracle in itself. I couldn't remember the last time I didn't at least have one small nightmare. He was helping me in so many more ways than he could even know.

I stepped out of the bathroom to find him sitting on the bed's edge with the sheet covering him from the waist down. It was a very inviting sight. He crooked his finger at me to come to him. It didn't take any thought to do what he wanted. I sat down beside him and he pulled me in for a hug. The kiss promised what would come next. Not really wanting to, I pulled away and laughed.

"We will never leave this bed if you keep doing that." I giggled as he reached for me.

"I'm okay with that," he grumbled. I feigned to fight him off and stood.

"I would be, too, but I would like to see some of St. Augustine while on this little vacation. We don't know how long we are here for." Saying the words aloud made me sad. It was the truth, though. We really didn't know. "Plus, I never called Shelly or Grandma yesterday to let them know we made it here safely. They're both going to be pissed." Another thought came to me. "Oh, and we have to go turn that earring in to the police station. I'm sure whoever it belongs to would like to have it back."

He laughed at the way I was rushing to relay everything. Finally, he stood, the sheet sliding away. He was naked before me. My mouth went dry. He looked like a Greek God with all of his perfectly chiseled features. I inspected him and noticed a scar on his chest. I made a mental note to ask him about it some other time.

"So, how about we save the Chief's water bill and take a shower together?" He stepped toward me with a predatory look about him — and I was his prize. He reached for me again and I yelped as I ran into the bathroom. Donovan was right on my heels.

He showed me again how much he loved my body. He

snatched the washcloth away from me and gingerly washed my body. We took turns doing that until neither of us could stand it any longer. We made the best of our shared shower. However, I don't think we really saved any water.

We decided the first stop on our tour of St. Augustine would be The Fountain of Youth. It was a beautiful piece of land with a ton of history. We took plenty of pictures and I was in awe of the beauty of it all.

We walked the grounds, hand in hand and discovered a group of peacocks. There was one who seemed to be a loner. The peacock came up to us. He fluffed his feathers out, made a horrible sound, and pecked Donovan in the butt. Donovan yelled and ran away as the bird followed right behind him, hot on his heels. I couldn't help the giggle that escaped my mouth, then I just laughed outright at him, as he was telling to bird to shoo. It was one of those scenes you wished you had a video camera. I was still laughing when one of the guides came and ushered the bird to where the others were. Donovan, hurt pride and all, walked slowly back to me, rubbing his backside, shaking his head.

"You think that was funny, huh?" He teased as he started to tickle me. I squeaked and ran from him. He had no problem catching up to me and wrapped his arms around me. He kissed my neck, and we gazed at the scene in front of us.

"This place really is nostalgic, isn't it? It's so beautiful," I murmured.

"It is beautiful, but you make it a complete picture." God, he is just so perfect, even when he was being cheesy.

"You are so sweet. Thank you," I replied as I turned to him and kissed him.

"I only speak the truth," he said before kissing the tip of my nose, then pulling me toward the exit. I guessed he was done with The Fountain of Youth tour. I still had to stop myself from laughing at the memory. He was never going to live this down. As we were walking to the car, my phone rang. It was my grandma. Shit. I still hadn't called her.

"Hey, Grandma. Sorry I haven't called you yet. Things got a little busy." I glanced over at Donovan and smiled. He winked back at me.

"Oh, honey, I'm just glad you're okay." She sounded terrified, her breaths coming in short pants. It sounded like she had just ran a marathon race.

"Why wouldn't I be? What's the matter Grandma?" I asked, a little nervous by her tone. She was silent for a little bit but I could still hear her breathing, so I knew she was there. "Grandma? What's going on?"

"Someone broke into your apartment." She paused. "They destroyed everything. The police said it didn't look like they took anything. You still have a lot of valuables, even if they are broken. Oh honey, I'm so sorry to call you and tell you this bad news over the phone!" As the words sunk in, I almost dropped the phone. I felt the familiar panic set in and I started to shake. Donovan looked at me questioningly. I put my finger up, to tell him one minute. He put his arm around me.

"Do they know who it was? They didn't take anything? Maybe I should call the police department. Actually, why didn't they call me? Or Donovan? They know he is with me." Anger surged up in place of being afraid. It was a more welcome emotion.

"They have been trying to call you both all day, honey. When they couldn't get a hold of either of you, they called me. Angel, Shelly's place was broken into as well, same scenario," she explained. I felt the blood drain from my face. There was only one person who would have done this: Abe. I had no other enemies. How had he figured out where we lived? Was Grandma safe by herself at her house?

I thanked her for calling me, told her I loved her, and ended the call. Donovan's phone rang at that instant. He walked away as he talked to whoever it was. His voice was low so I couldn't hear what he was saying, but I could see his jaw twitch. He tensed right up. I leaned up against the car and waited for him.

"Alright, see ya," he said as he walked back to where I was. I could tell by the look of fear in his eyes he was talking to someone from the police station. "I have your grandma's place under constant surveillance. She will be safe." I swear this man could read my mind. I nodded. "Are you okay?"

"I can't believe this is happening. How is it he can escape, destroy not one, but two homes, and still be on the loose?" I questioned, only half expecting Donovan to be able to answer.

"He is like a damned rat. He disappears any time we get near him. He did that when we were investigating him for the human trafficking, as well." He was angry. I was, too, but I didn't have it in my heart to take it out on Donovan. He was no longer just a police officer in my mind. Plus, he saved me and Shelly when this all went down with Abe and he was saving me now. He opened his arms and I went to him. "It'll be okay, Angel. I won't let anyone hurt you again." I truly wanted to believe him, but my body was still quaking in fear.

# CHAPTER NINE

Donovan thought it would be best if we relaxed on the beach for the rest of the day. It was a great idea and helped a lot with my nerves. The sun and the sounds of the ocean did wonders for my soul.

I called my renter's insurance company to set up an appointment for an appraisal. Thankfully, they would cover the cost of anything missing or broken.. I still couldn't understand how Abe our addresses, so I asked Donovan.

He shook his head and grimaced disgustedly. "Well, when the court documents were sent to his attorney," he growled. "Your addresses would be listed on them. However, as the victims of his crime, your addresses should have been blacked out. I'll have to find out who was responsible for that little error."

"I guess that makes sense. I can't believe he actually had the balls to go to our places knowing everyone is already looking for him." I voiced my opinion. "He is either really stupid, or crazy. I'm putting my money on the latter." I sat down on the blanket Donovan had laid out for us.

"I really hope they get him soon. I can't handle living in fear like this. I feel like I'm the one who is in prison, not Abe. It's so frustrating, and my mind doesn't know how to handle it. I don't know if I should be scared, angry, or depressed."

"You don't need to be afraid, or depressed. I don't break promises, and I told you I wouldn't let any harm come to you," he said as he sat down behind me, pulling me in between his legs. He put his arms around me and rested his chin on my shoulder.

I could be with him for an eternity. As the thought came to my mind, I pushed it away. I was in no way ready for an long-term relationship with Donovan. Yes, he is an amazing man, and great in bed, but I was still extremely messed up. If I can't even sleep at night alone, or feel secure enough by myself, how could I ever feel secure in a relationship? I've always refused to be one of those "clingy" females. Most of my past relationships didn't last because I wouldn't let go of my independence enough. Men, I guess, like to be needed.

"Penny for your thought?" he whispered in my ear.

"You don't want to know, believe me," I shot back over my shoulder and stood . I didn't really want to have this talk just yet. The afternoon was so calm, even if my mind wasn't.

He jumped up and was right in front of me before I knew it. He softly put his hand on my cheek, and lifted my face up so he could look in my eyes.

"Try me," he said.

I glanced at my feet and shook my head.

"I can't, Donovan. I just can't," I mumbled. My throat tightened. A tear escaped and rolled down my cheek. He lifted my chin and wiped the tear away. I looked into his eyes, and saw an unfamiliar emotion in them. The waterworks came. He pulled me into his arms and held me while sobs wracked my body. He held me like that until they finally subsided.

I sniffled and laughed as I pulled back from him.

"Well, I guess there goes my strong woman façade." He pulled me close again, but I didn't have it in me to pull away again.

"Are you kidding me? You are the strongest woman I have ever known in my entire life. Have you not sat down and thought about your past, actually thought about it, and what you have accomplished in that time? I wish you could see yourself from my point of view, Angel. Not many people can say they have almost received their Masters degree, along with working full-time, let alone what you have been through in the past month alone. Most people would be hiding away in their homes and not facing the world outside. Not you, though. Not my Angel."

The way he said 'Not my Angel' made my heart both soar and sink at the same time. Did he want me to be his Angel? I should tell him now I simply could not be the person he thought I was. Here he was, trying to make me feel better, when, every day he puts his life on the line to save others. I went to school and was a server at a small diner. Nothing heroic about that.

"Donovan, I have issues. I can't seem to sleep without having the most awful nightmares. Last night, I dreamt Abe shot you in the head, he disappeared, and I was the one who was left holding the gun. Then, you disappeared, and it was Ben on the floor. It was terrifying." I shuddered as a huge chill coursed from the top of my head, to the tips of my toes. That nightmare was the worst out of all of them thus far.

He grabbed my hands and looked me deeply in the eyes.

"I have nightmares too, Angel. They may not include you, but you've usually been in my dreams." He winked. then continued, "They can get pretty bad. I have nightmares where I am shot, some where I am the shooter, and many where my partner is lying in a pool of his own blood. My point is, having nightmares doesn't make you a bad, or weak, person at all. It doesn't make you crazy. It just means, sometimes, your subconscious is impossible to fight off." He stopped and thought for a minuteas if realizing something, "You dreamt Abe shot me? That must mean you worry about me, even just a little."

At that moment, my feelings for Donovan Mancini had grown so much I thought my heart would explode. This man was something else. I already could not imagine my life without him in it. I didn't want to depend on him, but I could feel myself falling in love with him, even though I had tried to fight it. The problem was, I didn't know how he felt about me. Yet at the same time, I wasn't sure I wanted to admit to myself how I felt about him.

"You're right. Nightmares don't mean that I'm crazy, but they do mean I have some seriously unresolved problems in here." I pointed to my head. "And yes, I do care about what happens to you. You have a dangerous job, and I have a very dangerous man out after me."

"I'd like to help you with that. Maybe, we can help each other," he said. He pulled me back down to sit on the blanket. "In the meantime, why don't we just enjoy the afternoon and relax?"

His idea of relaxing was making love on the beach. Of course, that obviously took my mind off of my current problems, which was fine with me. I didn't want to think about them anymore.

We went to the police station later and dropped off the diamond earring we had found the day before. The officer who took it said if it wasn't claimed within 30 days, it would become ours. I really didn't want it, even though it was extremely beautiful. I wanted the original owner to get it back. He or she was probably devastated when it was noticed missing.

A thought hit me. It's amazing that it was only a couple of days we had been in Florida. It felt like we have been here, together, for a very long time. That thought both scared, and excited me at the same time. I looked at Donovan and smiled. He smiled back and winked at me.

We went back to the condo, where I fell asleep, almost immediately, in his arms. I couldn't imagine feeling any better than I did at that moment. If only it didn't have to end…

# CHAPTER TEN

I awakened to my phone ringing. In the dark, I groggily reached for it, noting the unknown number. Thinking it may be the police calling again, or the insurance company, I answered.

"Hello?" I said in mid-yawn. In the darkened room, the clock glowed 4:10.

"Hey there, bitch." My blood ran cold and I sat straight up, fully awake. I knew that voice. It was burned into my memory.

"Abe? What do you want?" I shook Donovan's arm and he awoke with a start.

"I'm going to find you, little girl. If it's the last thing I do, I will find you and by the time I'm done with you, you're going to wish I had killed you." There was silence. He had hung up. I sat there, staring at the phone in shock. I began to shake, dropping my phone.

"What's wrong, Angel?" Donovan asked. His hand gently stroked my arm. "Who was that?" This time with more concern in his voice.

"It was him... it was Abe," I whispered. He has my phone number, I thought. Great. How do these things keep happening?

"He said he was going to find me and make me wish he had killed me. I believe him."

Donovan jumped out of bed, turned on the light, and paced while dialing his phone. He walked out of the room and I could hear his muffled voice. I was left alone with my thoughts, which is obviously never a good thing.

I had a horrible feeling of dread. Obviously, Abe had no problems finding my address and phone number. It wouldn't be too difficult for him to find me now. I stood up, threw on my robe, and headed for the kitchen. I needed coffee. Coffee was what I always turned to when I had a problem I couldn't figure out. Even though I doubted coffee could help me this time, I decided to try it anyway.

Donovan walked in as I was adding the hot chocolate.

"He's really getting ballsy, now. I'm so sorry, Ang," he said as he walked up behind me. "This shit has got to stop. Now!"

"Yeah, that was the scariest phone call I have ever received." I turned around into his waiting arms. "What do we do now?"

"We do nothing. We let the cops do their job," he replied. "It's 4:00 in the morning, Angel. Are you sure you should be drinking coffee and…" He looked at the empty hot chocolate packet sitting on the counter and smiled. " Hot chocolate at this time? Really? You put hot chocolate in your coffee?"

I smiled sleepily up at him. "Yes, I don't like the taste of coffee. Yet I like how it wakes me up. You should try it with the hot chocolate sometime. It's really good." I fell silent. I couldn't help thinking about whether or not we should be sitting here, in Florida, talking about coffee, while this psycho was on the loose. I almost felt guilty about the good time I have been vacationing while a criminal is out there, who could be hurting some other poor, unsuspecting, woman.

"They will let us know if, and when, Abe gets caught, right?" I mused.

"Of course," he said incredulously. "I would hope we'd be the first on their call list. I imagine the Chief doesn't want us here any longer than necessary," he chuckled, trying to lighten the dark mood hovering in the kitchen.

"I guess I still just can't understand how something like this would happen. I mean, how does one escape while being surrounded by police?" Why didn't they tackle him or something? I didn't say the last part out loud because I didn't want to seem like an idiot, which I'm sure I would have.

"He knocked out the two officers who were guarding him. By the time the others noticed something was going on, it was too late. He was already gone." Donovan stirred hot chocolate to his coffee. I smiled. This was the first time I had told someone to try it and actually have them do it. Well, Donovan did. He took a sip. "This is actually not too bad."

"Told ya. So, if he gets caught..." I began.

"When he gets caught," Donovan interrupted.

"Okay, so when he gets caught, what happens then? Are they going to put him away forever, or does he still only get the original sentence?" I asked.

"Oh, no. He will have an escape charge and assault on a police officer added on top of everything else. He'll be lucky if he sees the light of day again." That made me feel a little better, even though at the moment it felt unlikely he would ever be captured.

I walked past Donovan, toward the bathroom. I needed a shower to wash away all of these horrible, negative thoughts on my mind. I have always been one to worry about everyone else. I was afraid of losing the people I loved, since I had lost both of my parents at such a young age. I never really had any fear for myself until these last few weeks. This was a whole new feeling for me — fear. I was genuinely afraid for my and Shell's safety.

After my shower, I joined Donovan on the couch and we

watched movies. He even watched a chick flick with me, without one complaint. Could this guy be any more perfect? We scrounged around the kitchen and found some things to fix, and ate in silence, each of us deep in our own thoughts. Once we were finished, we went back to our designated spots on the couch, and watched two more movies. I wished that every day could be this boring, I thought. It wasn't even really boring, honestly, just relaxing.

I wondered, suddenly, if Abe had called Shelly. I grabbed my phone and dialed her number. She answered right away.

"Hey, Ang," she said. "Did he call you, too?"

"Yeah. I was wondering if he called you. This guy is crazy, Shell. I am genuinely afraid right now."

"I know! They need to hurry up and catch him so we can get back to our normal lives. I can't do this anymore," she whined. I hated when she used that tone. It was like nails on a chalkboard to me.

Wow, I was really being bitchy. It was either the stress, or the lack of sleep, or both. Either way, I needed to get over myself, and fast.

"They really do. I'm tired of living like this, too. I mean, the vacation is great and all, but I want my freedom, as well." I half whined myself. Did that tone seriously just come out of me? "Anyway, what have you been up to?" I had to change the subject.

"Oh, not much. Just getting some sun, and worrying sick about you and this messed up situation we have found ourselves in," she replied. "What about you? How is it going with your policeman?" I could hear her smiling, literally.

"He's not 'my policeman', Shelly," I chastised, but smiled at the thought. "We have been having a great time, though. He's a great guy."

"Have you slept with him?" Leave it to Shelly to move beyond being blunt. I shook my head.

"Shell!!!" I yelled into the phone and blushed.

"You did! You little slut!" She whispered loudly, laughing. I could not hide anything from her, not that I really wanted to. I had to talk to someone about my relationship with Donovan, or whatever it was. I guess the fact I could never lie to her comes from being best friends for so long. I smiled.

"Anyway... Have you met any hunky beach bums or surfers yet?" I asked, changing the subject to her favorite; all about her. That's right, I can quickly turn the tables around on her.

"Well, there's this one guy I met on the trail I was running on the other day..." she began. I already knew how that probably ended — with a very happy ending. I laughed out loud at that thought. Shelly can call me a slut all she wanted, but at least I waited a few days before sleeping with Donovan.

"Good, Shell. That makes me happy," I said, and I meant it. I was always glad to see her happy, in a relationship or not. "Well, hun, I'm going to get off of here and try to get some sleep. I need a nap," I laughed.

"Okay, Ang. I'll talk to you soon. Keep in touch, okay?" she asked.

"Of course. You too," I said, thinking about the fact that I had been the only one who kept in touch for a while now. I didn't want to start an argument, so I let it go. "Love you."

"Love you too, to the moon and back," she said and it made me grin as I hung up. She hadn't said that in years.

I looked up to see Donovan staring at me, smiling. "It's good to see you laughing," he said as he walked over to sit next to me.

"Shelly can be silly sometimes," I said.

"So, I'm not 'your policeman,' huh? I'm sorry, but I couldn't help but overhear that." He pulled my feet onto his lap and started to massage them.

"Mmm... That feels good..." I murmured. "And technically,

no. You're not 'my police man.'" I closed my eyes and let myself relax enough to enjoy the massage.

"Would you like for me to be? Your policeman, I mean?" he asked.

My eyes shot open and I looked at him, hard. What? I didn't know what to say to that. Of course, I wanted him to be mine. Or did I? I didn't know.

"What do you mean?"

"Well, I've been thinking, and I really like what we have going here. I haven't been able to get you out of my mind since the night we found you in that motel room. I enjoy spending time with you, and our intimacy... well... it's indescribable. That much, even you can't deny," he said and pulled me closer to him.

"No, I definitely won't deny that," I giggled, then grew serious. "As far as the rest, are you saying you want to start a relationship with me?"

"That's exactly what I'm saying, Angel. I know it may seem too soon, but I personally don't care. It seems like I've known you forever. How do you feel about it?" he asked.

How did I feel about it? Was I ready for a relationship right now? If I were, Donovan is the only man I wanted it to be with. But what if it didn't work out? Could my heart handle that kind of pain? I didn't think so. Not at this very moment.

"Umm... I... Well, Donovan, I really like you. Actually, I have developed some strong feelings for you. The problem is, I have some issues I have to work out. Baggage I'm not sure you'd want any part of, really," I said as I looked straight into his mesmerizing eyes.

He put his arms around me, and held me tight, as if he were afraid to let me go. If I were to be honest with myself, I'd admit I didn't want him to ever let me go, either. This whole thinking thing was going to be the death of me, if Abe didn't find me first.

"I'm willing to go any speed you need to. I don't want to rush you into anything you don't want to do. I could help you work through what is bothering you." He kissed the top of my head before loosening his grip on me. "You don't have to decide right now. I'll give you all of the time you need," he said and stood.

"Thank you, Donovan. You are such an amazing guy. I would like nothing more to take this farther — someday. I just don't want to scare you away with all of my drama," I said as I slowly got off of the couch and headed to the bedroom. It was getting late, and my eyes were starting to feel heavy. He stood in the doorway, blocking my entrance.

"There is no way that you could scare me away," he said and then kissed me with a desperation so deep I could feel it clear to my bones. I could never deny this man. I knew it already, but he didn't. However, I didn't think it would take him very long to figure it out.

# CHAPTER ELEVEN

What was that annoying sound? Was I ever going to be able to sleep a full night again? Now that the nightmares have subsided for the time being, other forces don't want me to sleep. I glared at the clock on the stand. 2:32 A.M.

The beep again. It was my phone. I had a text message. I knew I should've turned my phone on silent for the night, I thought, shaking my head. I swiped the screen to unlock the phone, and opened the message.

I dropped my phone as soon as I saw it. I quickly looked over at Donovan, who was still sleeping soundly. I got to my feet and picked the phone up off of the floor. I looked at the message again. I swear my heart stopped. It was a picture of my grandma. She was bound and gagged. You could tell she was pissed. She was glaring, but there were tears on her face as well. Below the picture, the words read:

*"Your granny isn't as feisty as you are. She won't be as fun to get rid of. If you want to see her alive again, come to her place. ALONE. If you bring the cops, or even call them, I will kill her. If you even tell that pig boyfriend of yours, I'll kill her. Think of something to tell*

*him so he doesn't try to come here looking for you. Text this number back with a time you'll be here."*

I could barely read the last part of the text for the tears streaming down my cheeks and the quivering of my hands. Abe had Grandma. Oh my God. What was I going to do? I couldn't tell Donovan. I couldn't call anyone. I had to do what Abe wanted or he was going to kill her. My heart broke. . I wasn't willing to take that chance.

I stood up and, as quietly as possible, walked to the condo's living room. Using my phone and an online airline site, I booked the first plane to Ohio. . I called a cab to take me to the airport. I sent the text to Abe telling him when I'd be there. I went to the kitchen to jot a note to Donovan. It was short, like the life of our relationship. It was killing me to write it. I truly hoped he would be able to forgive me.

> *Donovan,*
>    *I'm so sorry to leave you like this, but I couldn't stay any longer. Our conversation last night proved to me that I can't be in a relationship. Not with you, or anyone else. I'm sorry. Please forgive me.*
> *Angel*

I placed the letter on the kitchen counter, beside the coffee pot with a packet of hot chocolate to hold it down. The cab pulled up and walked out the door to it..

My plane landed in Ohio two hours later. I barely remembered the flight. I took a taxi to my grandma's house — a half hour drive. I wracked my brain, trying to think of how I was going to save Grandma — and get out of this alive myself. I came up blank. I couldo only hope he would at least let her go in exchange for my own life. Somehow, I doubted that would happen.

The cab pulled up in front of my grandma's house. Everything seemed so normal when I looked at the front of her place. I could see the television flickering through the window. I looked down the street. She lived in a quiet neighborhood, one which pretty much only had elderly people living in it. This was a crime free area. It saddened me to think that, after today, everything was about to change for this neighborhood.

I stepped out of the car and walked up the steps. As I reached for the handle, the door flew open, and I was yanked inside. My purse went flying across the room. I found myself on the floor, looking up. . Someone kicked me in the ribs. I saw him.

"Abe," I choked out as I gasped for air.

"Hey, Angel. Nice of you to join us. Right on time, too. Such a good girl. Our party was getting quite boring until you showed up." He kicked me again. I grunted..

"Where's she at? Grandma?" I called out and tried to stand up. I heard a muffled cry come from the next room. I looked and saw my grandma, her eyes wide, shaking her head.

"Why don't you let her go? I'm here now, you've got me. She doesn't need to be involved anymore. Please, just let her go." A small part of me hoped t he would listen to me and let her go. He laughed. It was an evil laugh.

"What? Do you think I'm stupid? Let her go, why? So she can go straight to the police? Yeah… Right…" Abe's hand went up into the air, a fist came down to my right jaw, effectively knocking me out.

I was on the beach again, holding hands with Donovan. The sky was blue, the ocean wind blowing through my hair. A dark cloud appeared above us. The wind picked up, whipping my dress and hair wildly. I looked at Donovan, worrying about the sudden change in weather. He evaporated in front of my eyes. I called for him, but received no response My ribs started to hurt, very badly. I doubled over in pain. That's when I realized — I wasn't dreaming.

I woke up tied to a chair, no idea how long I had been knocked out. Everything hurt. A familiar panic started to bubble up again. Abe was sitting directly in front of me. Watching… Waiting… I tried to focus beyond the pain in my ribs and jaw. Abe stood up and slapped me. I glared up at him through my tears. Wow, wasn't he such a big man, hitting women? Especially women who were tied up, completely unable to defend themselves. Bastard.

"What do you want from us, Abe?" I scanned the room, looking for Grandma. She was in the corner, crying silently, staring at me. She cringed when she watched him approach me . He knelt down until he was nose to nose with me. I smelt his breath and felt his spit on my lips as he talked.

"I told you what I wanted the other day when I called you, you dumb bitch. I told you I was going to make you wish you were dead. You killed my buddy, got me shot, arrested, and now it's time to pay up." He grabbed my hair, yanked my head back until my neck cracked. He forced a kiss on my mouth. It was bruising and I could taste the blood in my mouth when he bit my lip. I tried to pull away but he grabbed the back of my head so I couldn't move an inch.

Tears started and I was angry at my weakness. When he finished punishing my mouth, I glared at him. He backhanded me so hard, he knocked me over, chair and all, toppling to the floor.

"Don't you ever look at me like that again, bitch. He feigned another slap. "I'll knock your ass into next Tuesday. Do you understand me? This is your own damned fault. You put yourself in this position, *Angel*." He slurred my name mockingly, and with disgust. I noticed his eyes. The pupils were huge with no color to his eyes at all. Just black. He must be on something, I thought.

That or possessed by the Devil himself. That thought terrified me even more. I decided, right then, I needed to appease him, make him happy, even for a little bit to buy some more time.

"You're right," I whispered, "I'm sorry."

He grabbed me and the chair to set us up straight. It was like a switch had been flipped. He didn't look at me with so much hatred.

"Yeah, it's cool, but if you do it again, you're going to regret it." He glanced at my grandma. "So is your beloved granny. Don't say I didn't warn you."

I looked past him so I could see Grandma. She had her chin held high, even though she was crying. *I wish I had half of the strength that woman has,* I thought with pride. I almost smiled, until I remembered our predicament. I don't think Abe would appreciate a smile from me right now.

"Okay. I won't do it again, I promise."

He walked away, into another room, and left me alone. I was thankful but apprehensive at the same time. Who knew how long it would be before he decided to come back and deliver another blow? I looked over at my grandma again, and our eyes met. I just shook my head and smiled, attempting to let her know that everything would be okay. She, of course, knowing me better than I knew myself, knew I was just trying to make her feel better. We both were quite aware I was probably going to die. It was only a matter of time.

I heard muffled music coming from the other room and recognized it immediately. It was my cell phone. *Damn it.* I meant to shut if off before I got out of the cab. I didn't want Abe to know I had it, just in case I actually got the opportunity to escape him. I heard him curse, then a crash. The ringing stopped. Abe must have found the phone and smashed it. *Damn, damn, damn…* I leaned my head back, pissed off at myself.

I heard Abe stomp across the floor of the other room. He stood in the doorway for a moment, as if contemplating his next move. He stormed toward me until he was next to me.. Strangely, he sauntered to my grandma and slapped her across the face. The force threw her head back. My heart stopped.

"NO!" I screamed. I swore, if he touched her one more time, I'd find a way to get loose and kill him myself. "Don't punish her for what I did. Please, Abe. Punish me! I had to use the phone to text you and tell you when I'd be here. I just forgot to leave it somewhere else, like you wanted. You have to understand, it has kind of been a stressful day." I tried so hard to explain.

"Well, you see, Angel, by punishing her, it hurts you, too. I like to watch you suffer. I can see the pain it causes you when I hurt someone you love. Two birds, you know what I mean?" He smiled as he walked back to me. This guy is just sick, I thought. There was no way Grandma and I were going to make it out of this alive. I couldn't handle watching him hurt her anymore, though. I needed to bring his anger back toward me. If I can do something to piss him off enough... An idea came to me.

"She didn't do anything to you, though. She's innocent in this," I whispered. The tears were back as I watched my grandma's head bob up and down, almost passing out from the strike he delivered to her.

"Ha!" he laughed, mockingly. "There's no such thing as an innocent woman. Women do nothing but lie and cheat. Then they get all emotional when a man reacts to such treatment. Do you have any idea what it feels like to have someone you care about treat you like a piece of shit? No, probably not. You've probably been fed with a silver spoon your whole life." I didn't care what some woman he thought he loved did to him. It still was no excuse, in my eyes, to do these despicable things to another human being.

"You're wrong, Abe. I haven't had the best of lives. You have no idea what I've been through. I've been through hell before I was even a teenager. Besides, we aren't those women," I said, trying still, so hard, to remain calm. "We didn't do those things to you. We didn't lie, or cheat on you."

He took another cheap shot at my grandma, this time knocking her into the corner of the wall. I held my breath, trying to calm myself down before I did something stupid to get us both killed. Every fiber in my body wanted to kill him with my bare hands. I couldn't remember ever being so angry at a person. Not even Ben had instilled so much rage in me when he tried to kill me.

"You didn't lie, no, but you cheated me out of the money I was supposed to make off of your slut of a friend." He moved closer to me with each word. "Plus, you cheated me out of a life of freedom. You're not supposed to be alive right now, you bitch!" he screamed. Like a fury, he turned, scampered across the open area to lean over my grandma. He grabbed her by her chin and forced her face to look at him . He lifted her head and I saw the blood coming out of her mouth and nose. That was my last straw.

"You hate women so much that you would pick on a poor, defenseless, old lady? I thought you were more of a man than that," I screamed, knowing it was a mistake. I was going to pay for that statement. However, I needed him more angry with me so he would hopefully leave my grandma alone. I would never forgive myself for her being hurt. She didn't look like she could take one more strike.

He charged me and cut the ropes around my hands. Before I knew what was happening, he picked me up by the front of my shirt. He threw me on the ground, straddled me, and wrapped his hands around my throat. His fingers squeezed tighter. I tried to stop him. I grappled at his hands, and stretched to reach his face. I tried everything in my power to get him to stop choking me. However, he was just too big and strong. He overpowered everything I attempted.

"You're fucking done, bitch. I'm not playing any more games with your dumb ass. I don't even know why I've kept you around this long." He applied more pressure to my throat.

Well, this is it, I thought. This is the end; how you will die, Angel. I thought of all of the things I hadn't had a chance to accomplish in my life, nor would I get the chance to. No marriage, no kids, no career. Hell, I didn't even get to finish my Master's degree. I thought about Donovan, and the relationship we had just started. And how I ended it with a lie. I hoped he would be able to forgive me once he found out the truth.

"Please," I squeaked out.

"No. Fuck you. You're dead, and then it's on to dear old granny over there," he growled. "All you had to do was mind your own damned business, but nooo.... You couldn't do that, could you? You had to go and ruin everything I had worked so hard for. Now it's time for my revenge, bitch."

His voice was already starting to fade and the room was getting darker, and darker.

BANG!

Something heavy hit my chest. There wasn't any pressure on my neck, but I still couldn't breathe. It felt like an elephant was sitting on me. I started to cough. Air was being allowed in my lungs, but I couldn't get enough in to do me much good. The weight suddenly lifted off of me. I coughed repeatedly until I was dizzy.

"Angel!" I heard my grandma scream. I looked at my chest, and looked to see where Abe went. He wasn't anywhere around. I saw blood. A lot of blood. I didn't see or hear anything else. The room went dark.

# CHAPTER TWELVE

I was walking a familiar trail along the beach. Everything appeared fuzzy until my brain registered where I was. How did I get here again? The temperature was perfect. The sun beat down on my shoulders. I was wearing a blue sundress that billowed in the ocean breeze. Ahead, down the beach, I could see a figure in a white dress walking toward me, her auburn hair blowing in the wind. As we neared, a feeling I knew her enveloped me. The familiarity was so intense it almost overwhelmed me. It was as if a thick fog had cleared, and I knew exactly who she was. It was my mom. I walked faster, not blinking, for fear she would disappear if I did. She was smiling at me as we came about five feet from each other.

I ran the rest of the way and hugged her. She hugged me back, tightly, and then stepped away. I had never seen a more beautiful sight than my mother standing in front of me. I started to cry happy tears. This was the first time I had dreamt of her and was actually able to touch her.

"Sweetie, you have grown into a beautiful young woman. I am so proud of you and your accomplishments," she said. She seemed so serene, so happy. Her voice was beautiful. She suddenly grew serious. "But you have to go back now, honey. You're not done making me proud, yet."

"But I want to stay with you, Mom," I complained. I had no desire to leave her, or this wonderful place. Everything seemed so perfect here. It was as if my life was complete, right at this moment.

"You have to go back, sweetie. You have many more things to do. There are people waiting for your return, who are very worried about you right now." She spoke sternly, but lovingly. I could feel the love pouring out of her to me. "You have to wake up, before it's too late. You have to wake up right now!" she said with more emphasis and panic.

I felt a rush of air. I wasn't warm any longer. I was actually very cold. Why is it so cold? I felt myself being picked up. Pain! I felt so much pain I had difficulty breathing. I moaned loudly at the stabbing in my ribs. The moans threw me into a coughing fit, which intensified the pain. I truly hoped death didn't feel like this.

"Angel, can you hear me? Angel? Please, wake up. Don't leave me. Not right after I found you." The vague voice was a familiar, masculine.

"Donovan?" I croaked . How did he get here? Was I still dreaming? In a way, I hoped I was so when I woke up, the pain would end. At the same time, though, what if Abe would be there when I woke up again?

"Yes," relief flooding his voice. "It's me, Ang. Can you open your eyes for me, babe?"

I did what he asked and could see him hovering over me. He was smiling, but I could see the concern in his eyes which were wet with tears. That's when I remembered everything that had happened. It all came rushing back to me.

"Oh. My. God! Grandma?" I had to find her and tried to sit up. The pain flattened me right back out. All air left my lungs as the wind was knocked out of me. "Donovan, where's Grandma?" I whimpered. "Is she alright? He beat her so badly."

"Be still, Angel. You're hurt pretty bad. Your grandma is pretty beat up, too, but she's going to be okay. She's being looked at by one of the medics. You really had me scared there for a minute. I thought I lost you. We couldn't find a pulse." I looked back at him, relaxing a little, knowing my grandma was okay. Not that I would believe him fully until I saw her for myself. I scanned Donovan's face and noticed he had tears falling from his eyes. I reached to wipe one off, but gingerly because even that hurt. .

"Don't worry about me," I whispered. "You can't get rid of me that easily." He laughed at that, and then was pushed aside by one of the medics who put me on a back board. He and another medic lifted me up on a gurney. Donovan followed as they wheeled me out to the ambulance. Oh, great, another hospital stay for me, I thought. Then something struck me.

"Where's Abe?" I began looking, nervous again. "Did he get away?" I asked. That thought scared the hell out of me. I couldn't imagine having to go through something like this again, or having any other woman dealing with him.

"No, Angel," Donovan answered quickly. "He didn't get away. You won't have to worry about him . Ever." His words came to me through a fog, my eyelids grew extremely heavy. The medicine the medics put in my IV must have been pretty potent. I'd just take a little nap. Yes, sleep is good…

That was the last thought I had for next 12 hours. I awoke to Donovan sleeping in the chair beside my bed, Shelly sitting by the window, and my grandma walking into the hospital room. The room was white, but the lights were dimmed down, probably so I would sleep. When my grandma saw my eyes open, she ran up and sat beside me on the bed, almost kicking Donovan in her rush. The familiar smell of cherry jelly beans, the scent of her from my childhood, tickled my nose.

I didn't miss the black eye and swollen cheek on her face. I felt my eyes start to tear up at the sight. That son of a bitch. I hope he pays for the things he did to her, I thought. My grandma touched my cheek and wiped my tears. I flinched a little at the touch. I guess she wasn't the only one with a swollen face.

"Oh, honey, don't you dare cry for me. I'm just fine. Thanks to your man over there," she whispered as she nodded toward Donovan. " We both are going to be okay."

"What do you mean? What happened? The last thing I remember is Abe's hands around my neck and I couldn't breathe." I frowned, remembering his hands disappearing, but that was it. I reached up and touched my throat unconsciously. It was, of course, tender.

"When he had you on the ground, and was on top of you..." She shuddered. "Oh, it's just so hard to think about it. Anyway, Donovan came crashing through the door, like a knight in shining armor, and shot that big, horrible, man." Grandma looked over at Donovan with admiration in her eyes.

"Donovan shot him?" That must have been the heavy weight on my chest when the hands disappeared suddenly. I remembered all of the blood. I knew it couldn't have been mine, so it must have been Abe's. I swallowed, the nausea threatening to show its ugly face.

Donovan woke up at that moment and leaned over toward me. He ran his hand through his hair and rubbed the sleep out of his eyes. There were horrible, dark circles under them. He grabbed my hand in between his and kissed the tips of my fingers.

"Yes," he said, "I shot him. When I came in the house and saw him on you like that — I saw red and lost it." His face reddened in anger and fear.

"Thank you for saving me, again," I whispered as he leaned in to kiss my forehead. That hurt, too. What the hell did Abe do to me? I didn't think there was a spot on my body that didn't hurt.

"You don't need to thank me, babe. I would do anything for you, and yes, that means I'd kill for you." He trailed his fingers up my arm, raising goose bumps in its wake.

"Kill for me?" I asked as the realization of what he had just said came over me. "He's dead?"

"Yep. He took a bullet to the heart."

"Oh."

Donovan had risked his life, and took someone else's, for me. Little ol' me. Was I even worth all of that? I didn't think so, but it made me appreciate him that much more. My heart swelled, but my head hurt. I couldn't wrap my mind around all of the events that took place. I yawned, which made me flinch.

"You need to get some rest, Angel. We should leave you alone for a bit," Shelly piped in, causing me to jump. I almost forgot she was there. She walked over to me, patted my arm, and said, "Again, I am so sorry." I shook my head.

"Again, it wasn't your fault, Shell. You had no idea this was going to happen. Any of it," I reassured her. She had to stop blaming herself for everything. She smiled at me then stepped out the doorway.

"Shelly's right, honey. I think I'm going to go home for a bit and try to straighten up the mess that big oaf made of my house," Grandma said.

"I'm sorry, Grandma. I don't know how he figured out where you lived."

"First of all, it's not your fault, just like it's not Shelly's fault. Second, the house needed some renovations anyway. Now I have a reason to spend some money on new carpet and windows. The insurance company will take care of any damage done. Oh, and especially the front door," she said as she winked at Donovan. He smiled and moved to her spot beside me on my bed.

"I'll be back later to see you. Love you so very much, my Angel. Your momma would be so proud of you," Grandma said and slipped out. I didn't miss seeing the tears sneaking out of her eyes as she left. It was almost like *deja vu* hearing those words.

I shifted my attention back to Donovan. He was staring at me like he wanted to say something.

"I'm sorry I had to leave like that," I said and pushed the button to lift my head up a little on the bed. That didn't feel any better than yawning. "He told me if I told you, or anyone else, where I was going, he would kill Grandma."

"It's okay. I understand now since everything is over. You can imagine my shock when I discovered you weren't in bed with me when I woke up. But then when I read the note you left... I knew something was off." He stood up and walked over to look out the window.

"How did you figure it out? How did you find me?" I asked. He was like my own personal guardian angel, I thought. That made me smile a little on the inside. At least my guardian angel was hot. He let out a breath, like he was holding it forever.

"When I read your note, like I said, I knew something was very wrong. So, I called the airlines to see if you had booked any flights." He winked at me. "Being a cop has its major advantages. Anyway, I tried your cell a few times, and it went to your voicemail right away. You returned to Ohio, so I bought a matching ticket for the next flight. Upon landing a couple of hours later, I tried your phone again. When it rang, I was hoping you would answer. But you didn't. Someone did, but then I heard a noise. The call dropped."

That must have happened when Abe smashed my phone, I thought.

"After that, the bad feeling I had in my gut got way worse. At that point, I was terrified; desperate. I freaked out and called the Chief. I was running out of ideas, so I figured he'd shine some new light on everything." He walked back over and sat next me again. He took a deep breath, and let it out slowly as he watched my face. "He asked me if you had a newer phone, which you did. He then had the brilliant idea of checking your phone's GPS signal. It worked. Even though the phone wasn't working, the GPS still told us where it was located last. It showed your grandma's address. I was terrified. I knew something was very, very wrong at that point." His eyes started to water.

"It's alright, Donovan. I'm okay, thanks to you, and so is Grandma." I attempted to smile reassuringly, which caused my lip to sting.

"I know you're okay, but there's more to the story. When I got to the house, I had to wait for the other damned officers to show up for back up. It was the longest time of my life, Angel. Not knowing what was happening to you on the other side of that door was agonizing." He leaned in, and kissed me, ever so softly, then went on.

"Finally, the rest of the team showed, and we could strategize what our next move was going to be. I demanded on going in first, even though the Chief tried talking me out of it. He didn't want me to be the first to find you, if that asshole killed you." He shuddered at the memory. "Anyway, we blasted through the door, and that's when I saw you — on the floor, with that bastard on top of you. I shot him immediately. Abe was dead before he fell, but he dropped right on top of you. I grabbed him to get to you, but you weren't responsive. You were just lying there." He shuddered, placed his hand on my cheek and looked deeply into my eyes, as if he was searching for something.

"When I checked for your pulse, I couldn't find one. You

weren't breathing. It was the scariest moment of my life, Angel. I thought you were gone…" He looked away. I reached out and grabbed his arm. He turned back, tears streaming down his face.

"You saved my life, Donovan. I'm still here because of you. If you hadn't come when you did… I'm just lucky. It could have turned out so much worse. Abe had the perfect opportunity to do the most horrible things to me, but you stopped all of that from happening." I remembered an important detail about when I was out. "I dreamt of my mother. She told me I had to come back to you all. That it wasn't time for me to be with her yet. I'm not going to lie, I really didn't want to leave her," I uttered. Maybe it wasn't a dream after all. I never really believed in the whole 'light at the end of the tunnel' story people would tell after a near-death experience. I almost had to believe them now. Donovan stood up and leaned over me.

"Well, I'm glad your mother told you that you couldn't stay with her. I would never be able to smile again if you had. Look, I love you, Angel. I don't know how it happened so fast, but I do. I love you, and I can't picture my life without you in it. I won't, actually. There's nothing you can say or do to change my feelings for you," he said as he kissed the top of my head. Those three words made my heart monitor go off. I laughed, and flinched from the pain. Donovan smiled . "I guess my love hurts," he chuckled. He looked so exhausted.

"You should go and get some rest, Donovan. I'm sure I'm due for some more pain medicine soon, anyway, based on how I'm feeling right now. I'm okay, I promise. I'm not going anywhere," I assured him and smiled. He loves me, I thought. Wow.

"You better not go anywhere like that again, woman," he admonished. I gave him a stern look. "Okay, okay, I'll go," he said. "But I'll be back really soon. I have to go to the station and fill out paperwork anyway." He walked toward the door. I couldn't just let him leave like that.

"Donovan?" I called, and he turned around to face me. "I love you, too," I said.

He smiled and walked back to me, leaned over, and kissed me gently again, and then he was gone. He must have passed the nurse, because no sooner than he was out, she was walking in with my medication. Thank the heavens above.

"How are you feeling, Angel?" she asked as she was typing something on the keyboard of the computer.

"Like I've been hit by a truck," I replied, half joking. I'm pretty sure if someone were to live after being hit by a vehicle, this is exactly what it would feel like.

"Well, that happens when you've been through what you have, honey," she said as she started checking my vital signs. Even the blood pressure cuff hurt as it squeezed my arm. "You have three broken ribs, a bruised sternum I'm assuming from the CPR, a mild concussion, and some torn ligaments in your left shoulder. Also, you have bruises in places no one should ever have bruises," she said sympathetically. "Would you like some more pain medicine?"

"Yes, please," I almost begged. I normally hated pain medicine, because it made me feel loopy, but right now, I needed it. She picked a syringe up off of the counter, and put it in my IV. I felt relief almost immediately, which made me even drowsier than I was. I fell asleep . My last thought was that of Donovan loved me.

# CHAPTER THIRTEEN

T wo weeks in the hospital, I was beginning to think I was never going to go home. It felt like my entire summer was spent in a hospital room. I would be happy if I never had to see the inside of these walls ever again. Donovan stayed with me most of the time. We were watching some creepy show about insects invading people's homes, and bodies, when the doctor came in. Thankful for the interruption, and for saving me from nightmares about bugs, I gave him my full attention.

"Hey, Angel, how are you feeling today?" He listened to my lungs and heart with a stethoscope. He looked pleased with what he was hearing.

"Much better, thank you," I answered after I exhaled the deep breath I knew he expected of me. It was nice to not have that one small action hurt like hell. He felt along my ribs, shoulders, and pushed on my stomach a little, which only gave me minor discomfort. Compared to what I was feeling like two weeks ago, I could take it. Seemingly content with what he saw, he smiled.

"Great. Everything is looking, and feeling, just as it should. However, I want to get some more routine blood work. Then?" He shrugged. "I don't see any reason why you shouldn't be able to go home later today. You'll need to follow up with your family doctor, of course, but I think our job is done here at the hospital."

"Awesome! Thank you!" I practically yelled in my excitement at the news. He just chuckled, shook Donovan's hand, and walked to the door.

"You're a very lucky lady, Miss Brady," he said.

"So I've been told, and I am actually beginning to believe it, doctor. Thank you again," I said and he was off. I looked at Donovan and smiled. He sat down on the bed and kissed me.

"Finally," I murmured. "I didn't think they were ever going to let me get out of here."

"Well, you have been through hell, Ang. Your body really needed the time to heal," he said as he nuzzled into my neck. That gave me goose bumps. I couldn't wait to get out of here and get my life back on track. After arguing with Shelly for an hour about it, I finally talked her into bringing in my laptop and books so I could still work on my schooling. She didn't see why it was so important. I knew I didn't want to fall behind after everything else. If I failed my courses, then Abe would have won at destroying a part of my life. Alive or dead, I didn't want to give him any of that satisfaction. He didn't deserve any of it. Plus, I had nothing better to do, so I figured I may as well get caught up on that.

Suzy from work came to see me, bringing flowers and cards from all of the other employees at the diner. She couldn't wait to get me back to work. She said the diner was falling apart without me. I knew she was lying and just trying to make me feel better, because she could run that place completely by herself. That woman amazed me on a daily basis when I worked with her. The words, even if they were lies, made me feel needed, and I need that.

"I know my body needed to heal, and it has," I told Donovan, getting back to our conversation. My mind had a really hard time focusing on one thing at a time. "But I'm ready to get things back to normal, if that's even possible. I want to go back to work, and go to my classes. I want to be able to help Grandma pick out new paint and carpet for her living room. I needed to get out of this hospital. Also, I should probably call the therapist." I looked at him.. "The nightmares are back."

"I noticed. Some nights when I stayed with you, you moaned and thrashed about," he said as he gathered me in his arms. "It's so hard to see you go through something, in your sleep, and me not being able to do anything about it. It's a horrible feeling, being helpless when a loved one needs you the most." Those words almost broke my heart.

I snuggled into him, loving his scent. There really wasn't anything I didn't love about this man. He saved my life, twice, killed a man for me, and has been by my side through everything. The nurse came in from the lab, to draw blood, and interrupted my thoughts and snuggling. I blushed and gave her my arm. She was the best one to come in here from the lab so far. I barely even felt the needle and she was done really quick.

"These results should be back in no time. Then, it looks like you get to leave us." She smiled, took out my IV, put a bandage over it, and walked out.

"Well, I should probably go take a shower, and change into something other than this hospital gown. They just don't make these in my color, and they do nothing for my figure," I said as I started to stand up. I must have moved too fast, because if it weren't for Donovan holding me up, I would have fallen right on my butt. That was an odd dizzy spell. I hadn't had any since my first week at the hospital. I was suddenly nauseous.

"Whoa, Ang, are you okay?" he asked as he steadied me. "Do you want some help into the bathroom?"

"Ha, no, thanks. I'm fine. I just stood up too fast. I guess I've spent too much time lying in that bed." I reached for the bag he brought for me that had some of the things I had left in Florida in my rush to get to my grandma's. I made my way toward the bathroom, and turned on the shower.

"Hey, I'm going to go get some coffee, and pull the car around to the doors. Oh, and you make that hospital gown look good," he joked. "Take it easy in there. Don't be afraid to call one of the nurses in here if you get lightheaded again. Promise me," he called after I shut the door.

"I promise I'll pull the cord if it happens again. Honestly though, Donovan, I'm fine," I yelled to him. I started to feel nauseous, and my head was pounding at the same time. My stomach chose that moment to empty its contents. When I was finished throwing up, I stepped under the water of the shower. Donovan didn't say anything else, so I figured he had left the room. I was thankful, because there is nothing more embarrassing than throwing up in front of your boyfriend.

After I had finished my shower, which by the way, was the best shower I had ever taken. Well, besides the one in Florida, with Donovan, I thought, smiling at the memory. There was a knock on the door. It was the doctor. He had an interesting look on his face.

"Are you ready to release me, doc?" I asked, smiling hopefully while tying my robe.

"Yes, but there is something that I need to talk to you about, Angel," he answered as he sat down in the chair beside the bed, and looked at his paperwork. "Why don't you sit down for a second, so I can ask you a couple of questions?" He was studying my face extremely closely. He was waiting for me to say something.

Confused, and a little nervous, I sat down. What was wrong with my blood? Did I have cancer or something like that? My anxiety went through the roof.

"What's up?" I asked.

"Angel, when was your last menstrual cycle?" he asked, watching me. It was like he was expecting me to catch on to something. I had no idea what he was getting at.

"Umm... I don't know. I mean I guess I'm about due for it any day now. Well, I may be a few days late. Probably from the stress of everything..." I was rambling, trying to think. It wasn't working. My mind became a jumbled up mess.

"Okay, well, the reason I asked is because I ran a few tests on your blood. It's usually just as a precaution," he began. I was only hearing half of what he way saying. "A pregnancy test is one of those tests, and... well... your's came back positive." He waited for my reaction. I knew what he was waiting for. Panic set in.

"So... I'm pregnant?" The voice was mine but I couldn't believe I was asking. No way. How did I let that happen? This is what I get for not being the usual, practical Angel. This is what happens when I do things out of character, such as having unprotected sex. How would Donovan react to this news?

Everything was happening so fast as it was, and this was really fast. I didn't even know if Donovan wanted children. It's not like we really ever had the chance to talk about it. Did he even like kids? Sure, I wanted a couple, someday, but now? The timing couldn't have been more wrong. I wanted to focus on school, and deal with my personal issues, and now, this was another added issue. This was going to throw a wrench in my plans for life. This could either make, or break, Donovan and I. Well, I guess at least I knew why I was sick before my shower...

"Yes, you're pregnant, Angel. Are you alright? You're looking a little pale. Do you want me to get you a glass of water or something? Should I call someone?" The doctor asked questions. I heard him, but my own thoughts were much louder than his voice. "Miss Brady?" He started to stand, his hand reaching out to me.

I snapped out of my thoughts, and stood . Donovan would be expecting a text telling him they were wheeling me down soon, or I had no doubt he would be coming back up to see what was taking so long. He worried about me too much as it was. I could only imagine what he would be like if he knew I was pregnant with his baby. I could see him being border-line paranoid. I wanted to laugh out loud. My attention shifted back to the doctor, who was probably afraid the news threw me into shock, with me being so silent.

"I'm okay. That was just shocking information, that's all." I laughed nervously. "It seems I have a lot of things to think about. I can I go now?" I asked as I was gathering my things, blindly.

"You can go as soon as the nurse comes in with your paperwork. We will need a couple of things signed, like your release forms, and your after hospital at home care instruction," he said . "Are you sure you're going to be okay with the news? I can give you a list of doctors with whom you can set up a prenatal appointment. They will be able to tell you how far along you are. I can get you started on some prenatal vitamins. The sooner you start those, the better for both you and the baby. I will write you a prescription for them along with your other medications. Also, Angel, there are other options you have." He smiled and walked out, leaving me with my thoughts once more.

Other options? Like what? I realized what he meant. He was talking about abortion, or adoption. I had never been forced to make the decision before. I honestly didn't think I could ever have an abortion. However, I didn't know if I could carry a child for nine months, only to give him or her up at birth. No way. I wasn't going through either of those. I needed to talk to Donovan about this, and soon. I just hoped he wouldn't ask me to do something I would have to hurt him for.

Pregnant. Wow. That was definitely not what I was expecting

the doctor to come in and tell me. I liked to think I was a smart person, so why didn't I think to use protection with Donovan? I knew what could happen. I guess I just wasn't thinking beyond my hormones. I didn't think much at all when it came to Donovan.

The nurse walked in with my paperwork to sign. The post-care forms listed all of my injuries, and how to take care of them at home. As I was flipping through them, the last one was a list of prenatal doctors. There were a prescriptions for pain, and also prenatal vitamins. I took that prescription, and the last form with the list of prenatal doctors, folded them up, and put them in my jeans pocket. I thanked the nurse who smiled and said goodbye. I sent a text to Donovan, saying I would be on my way down in just a minute.

He was waiting by the car, out front, when I was wheeled out. I took a deep breath, enjoying the fresh air, and smiled at him. I would tell him about the baby later. I didn't have it in me to deal with a rejection, if he handed it to me, right now. He helped me into the car, threw all of my stuff into the trunk, and finally, we started for my apartment.

"How does it feel to be free?" he asked, smiling.

I smiled back, and closed my eyes.

"Refreshing. I was beginning to get claustrophobic in that room." I didn't look at him. Instead, I looked out the window. I was afraid. If I looked at him, he would know something was going on. I felt his hand on my leg and looked at it. It felt so normal. So right. I didn't know how I was going to approach him about this pregnancy. "Now let's go get something to eat. I feel like I haven't eaten in weeks. Of course, hospital food isn't really considered food, is it?" I laughed. I needed to get us to somewhere I didn't have to worry about anyone overhearing what we were talking about. Even though, by the time we got anywhere, I had no longer the guts to confess to him what I knew.

# CHAPTER FOURTEEN

"**Y**OU'RE WHAT?" Shelly screamed in my ear when I told her about the pregnancy. I cringed. I should have known she would react this way. She's such a drama queen.

"You heard me. I'm pregnant." I was sitting on my couch, my legs curled under me, hugging a pillow. I knew Shelly would act like this, but my grandma, I was pretty sure, was going to kick my ass. She would be disappointed in me, I was sure of it. That thought broke my heart.

"Holy shit, Angel! What are you going to do? Are you happy? Scared? What does Donovan think about it?" Her questions rushed at me.

"I… umm… haven't exactly told him, yet? I don't know what do, Shell. I never, in a million years, thought the doctor would come in and tell me something like that. I don't know how to feel about it. I wouldn't say I'm 'happy' about it. I'm actually terrified. I have no idea what kind of mother I will be. I wasn't planning on something like this happening for at least another five years. What am I going to do, Shell? Tell me what to do." I was panicking all over again.

"Well, you're going to have a baby," she said, while laughing. I'm glad she was getting a good laugh out of my situation, the little bitch. She was only amused because it wasn't happening to her. This is something everyone had thought she would go through. Not me. Never Miss Innocent Angel. I never took chances, never fell in love, and never had sex, unprotected. That was, until, I met Donovan. I smiled. She was lucky I loved her. "I guess, at least something good came out of this whole mess."

"Something good? I don't know about all that. What if Donovan doesn't even want any kids? I've never asked him before. We honestly never made it to those types of conversations. What if he rejects me and the baby? I couldn't do it alone." I had this image of me fighting with a child to get dressed every day, making huge messes while he or she was eating. Or attempting to go to the store… I had watched way too many moms with screaming kids, all because the kid didn't get the toy or candy they wanted at the time. Ugh! I shook my head. No, I most definitely could never raise a child by myself.

"I don't think Donovan would turn his back on you, no matter what, Ang," Shelly said. "He is so obviously, madly in love with you. He didn't leave your side the whole time you were in the hospital. Not to mention he saved your life. Hello?" She made perfect sense. All of what she said was the truth. It still didn't change the fact — we knew so little of each other.

"I hope so, but we are just so new. These types of things destroy relationships that are years into them. We have only been together for a month, Shell. One month. We barely even know anything about each other." It may have felt like I had known him my whole life, but the truth was, I hardly knew much about him other than his shoe size and what little bit he told me about himself. That thought made me want to laugh and cry at the same time.

"You'll be fine, honey," Shelly assured me. "He's not going to reject you, or this baby. You need to tell him, though. The longer you wait, the more upset I think he will be. I don't think he'll appreciate finding out about being a daddy when the baby is coming out." My phone chimed. I looked . It was Donovan calling on the other line.

"Oh, it's him. I'll call you later. Love ya!"

"Love you, too, Ang. Call me if you need anything. Oh, and I want to know when your due date is as soon as you find out. There are plans to be made." She continued to talk as I switched over to the other line.

"Hey," I said, answering Donovan's call.

"Hey, yourself," he replied. "What are you up to right now?" I heard him shut his car door.

"Nothing, really. Just getting caught up on some school work. I just got off the phone with Shelly. What about you?" I asked, getting up from the couch to pick up my used plate, from way earlier in the day, and take into the kitchen. I was getting pretty lazy these days.

"Well, I'm currently walking up to your door with your favorite Chinese dish. Want to let me in?" he asked.

The thought of Chinese had my stomach rolling and gurgling, and not in a good way. What a sweetheart, bringing me food and all. I didn't have the heart to tell him it didn't sound so good, so instead, I decided to go along with it.

"Okay. I'm coming." I walked to the door, waited for him to come into view of the peep hole, and opened it when I saw him. My heart started to pound familiarly, as it did every time I saw him. I hoped the feelings he brought me never went away, as it does with many other couples after time. Too many times, people fall in and out of love too fast.

He walked in, stopped to give me a peck on the lips, and went on to the kitchen. He started unpacking the food, and plating it up. I sat at the table, waiting for him. He put the plate in front of me. I smiled my thanks, but, as soon as the scent of it reached my nostrils, I was immediately nauseous. I stood abruptly, and ran to the bathroom to be sick. I was almost certain I was never going to want Chinese food again by the time I was finished. Just the thought of it had me gagging again. I pushed it from my head.

After washing my face, and brushing my teeth, I made my way to the couch, a little embarrassed. I couldn't go back into the kitchen, because I would get sick all over again if I smelled any of the food. Donovan stood and stood at the living room archway.

"Are you alright, babe? You don't look so good," he asked, his face full of concern. "You usually love Chinese."

I looked up at him as he approached me. He looked so sexy in his police uniform. Even after emptying the contents of my stomach, my libido was was able to go crazy every time I saw him. We hadn't been intimate since Florida because he was worried about hurting me. The things I could do to him right now.What the hell was wrong with me? Who thinks like that? Who was this woman I was becoming? I swear, I barely even knew myself anymore.

"I'm good," was the only thing t I could say. I couldn't exactly tell him what was going through my head right then, and I didn't know how to start to tell him why I was sick.

"Do you have a stomach flu or something? Or is it all of the medication? Maybe food poisoning?" he asked.

Now was the time. I had to tell him, especially if my stomach was going to be stupid every time he brought over Chinese food.

"Come and sit with me, Donovan," I said as I patted the seat next to me on the couch. "We need to talk." He sauntered over, and sat down.

"That's never what a guy wants to hear from his girlfriend.

'We need to talk' are the four words we all fear. That usually is followed by bad news," he said quietly, nervous.

"I'm sorry. I shouldn't have said it like that." I backtracked. It was too late to back out now. I had to tell him. I just didn't know how to begin.

"I mean, it wasn't supposed to come out like that. Okay, so here goes. Before I left the hospital, do you remember the doctor said he ordered some blood work?" I asked, gauging his reply. He nodded. I took a deep breath.

He was beginning to look concerned. "Is something wrong with your blood work?"

"No. Nothing is really wrong, so to speak. Well, little did I know, one of those tests was a pregnancy test. It came back positive, and apparently, I can't handle the smell of Chinese food right now." blurted it all in one breath. There. I said it. It was out. I watched him closely, waiting for it to all sink in. I was terrified. I wished I could read thoughts at that moment. Or maybe not…

He sat there staring at me for a very long time. He didn't say anything, I thought he was in shock from the news. I was about to say something else, to bring him out of his trance-like state, when he got up, turned his back to me and took a couple of steps away. Here it is, this is the part where he tells me he never wanted children, and now he never wants to see me again. My heart started to pound. He turned back to me and I noticed the small smile on his lips. That small smile turned into a huge grin as he took the few steps back to me. He knelt down in front of me, putting his hands on my knees.

"Are you serious?" he asked, incredulously. "You're pregnant? We're going to have a baby?" I nodded. He laughed. "When?"

"I don't know, yet. I have to make an appointment with one of the doctors on the list the hospital gave me." I was surprised by his sudden giddiness.

"Well, then we need to get on with it. Where's the list? We will start the process right now," he said as he stood again. He began pacing the room. "How do you feel about this? Are you okay?" he asked, as if remembering I may not even want kids myself.

"I don't know how to feel right now. I'm okay, but, it's so soon. You're not angry?" I asked quietly.

"Angry? Are you kidding me? This is amazing news!" He came back and snatched me up off of the couch. I squealed and he set me back down on my feet. "Oh, that was probably bad for the baby." I laughed at his new concern. My original thought about his being over protective of me and the baby returned.

"I don't think that picking me up is going to hurt the baby. I'm sure it takes a lot more than that," I said as I hugged him. I was totally relieved from his reaction to the news. "I thought you would be upset by this. I didn't even know if you wanted children, Donovan."

"I have always wanted kids. My ex and I tried, but she never got pregnant. Then she cheated on me and got knocked up by the other guy. I always thought there was something wrong with me, like I couldn't have any," he mused. He shook his head, as if clearing his mind of the thought, and looked back into my eyes. "I guess she just wasn't the right woman, and it wasn't meant to be. This is, though. We're going to have a baby?"

I nodded. "We're going to have a baby," I repeated, answering his question.

"Wow. This is great. Here I thought you were going to tell me you were done with me, or needed space, and you hit me with this...this... amazing news!" He laughed. "So, you've known since yesterday?" I nodded. "Why didn't you tell me then?"

"I was afraid to. I didn't know how you would react. I didn't know if you would be upset, happy, or What? This has opened my eyes to the fact we really don't know much about each other, Donovan," I said as I looked down at the floor.

He reached up and cupped my cheek. I leaned my head into his hand, reveling in the feeling. He knew exactly how to comfort me. He knew how to make everything okay.

"I know I love you, and that's enough for me. I also know you are to become the mother of my child, and that makes me love you that much more," he whispered before kissing me soundly.

"I love you, too." I whispered back.

Donovan slid his hand down to my stomach.

"I'm going to be a dad," he murmured, in awe about the whole thing. I smiled and laid my hand over his. I had no idea what kind of mother I would be, but at least I knew now I wouldn't be doing it alone.

He chose that moment to kneel on the floor, in front of me. He put his lips on my stomach and kissed it.

"Hey there, little guy. I'm your daddy, and I'm going to do everything it takes to keep you and your mommy safe. Oh, and I'm going to spoil you rotten," he said to my stomach, which made me laugh.

Donovan gazed up at me and smiled the biggest smile I had seen come from him, yet. My phone chose that moment to ring. I picked it up to see who was calling. It was Grandma. Perfect timing. I swear this woman has a sixth sense when it came to knowing exactly when to call me. I guess if I could tell Donovan about the baby, then I needed to tell Grandma, too.

"Hey, Grandma," I said after tapping accept.

"Hi, honey. How are you settling in? Are you feeling okay?" she asked. Such an amazing woman.

"I'm good, actually. Donovan just got here."

"Oh, well I can call you back if you want so you can spend some time with him," she said.

"No, it's okay. Actually, Grandma, I've been meaning to call you. I have to tell you something," I began. She was silent for a second.

"Okay. What's going on? Is everything alright?" Always the worrier, I thought. Of course, I knew this is where I got it from.

"Well, when I was being discharged from the hospital, the doctor came in and said he wanted to take some blood tests before I left," I started.

"Yes. I think they do that for everyone before they let them leave. I personally think it's the doctors hoping they'll find something else to charge you for." I giggled at her suspicious tone.

"Well, you see Grandma, they did find something else when they did my blood work," I continued.

"Oh, no, sweetie. What do you mean? What did they find in your blood?" I felt guilty as I realized she was panicking, thinking I had cancer or something.

"Nothing deadly, Grandma," I quickly added. "They found a baby."

"They found a baby in your blood? Oh! Wait… Oh! They discovered you're going to have a baby! I'm going to be a great-grandmother! Oh my!" she exclaimed. I let out a sigh of relief for the second time today. Not that I thought my grandma would ever turn her back on me, but I was still nervous she would be disappointed in me. She, after Shelly, would usually be the first to tell me when I was messing my life up, or doing something stupid.

"Yep. I'm going to be a mom. Donovan and I are going to be parents, and you are going to be a great-grandma. A young Great-Grandma, at that," I said as I glanced over at Donovan. His smile hadn't faltered at all since he found out that he was going to be a father. I smiled back at him.

"This is great, Angel," she started, but then grew silent for a second. "How do you feel about this? Are you okay with it?"

"Well, I was a bit shocked to learn about the baby, and this is seriously going to change things. Oh, I learned something new today. Apparently, Chinese food is no longer my friend. Anyway, yes, Grandma, I am actually pretty happy about being a mom. Donovan is happy, too."

"I would hope he'd be happy. He's going to have a baby with the most perfect woman in the world," she said with so much indignation, I had to laugh.

"Oh, Grandma, you crack me up. I'm going to let you go for now, okay? I'll call you tomorrow. I love you."

"I love you, too, my Angel. Oh, and congrats," she said, "You have made this old lady's night." My heart was bursting with all of the joy and love that filled my small apartment living room at that moment. After I hit 'end' on my phone, I looked back over to where Donovan was sitting beside me. He reached over and pulled me onto his lap.

"So," he began, "where do we go from here?"

"What do you mean?" I asked.

"Well, I can tell you I don't want to miss an appointment, and I want to help you with the doctor bills, and all of that stuff…"

"I wouldn't keep you from any doctor appointments, Donovan. As far as the bills, we can figure that out when the time comes," I answered.

"Where do you see us now? I mean, are we going to continue living separately, or are you going to let me talk you into moving in with me?" He watched me closely, gauging me. That came out of left field. Once I composed myself, I looked at him.

"Why does it have to be your place? Why can't you move in here, with me?" I half teased. Donovan looked around my small, one bedroom apartment. Of course he wouldn't want to live here. I had to stop myself from giving my inside joke away.

"We could live here, I guess, but my house has three bedrooms, and a great backyard, for the baby to play in," he said.

"I was joking, Donovan. Of course you wouldn't want to

move in here. My place is so tiny. Where would we put a baby?" I was laughing now. I stood up and looked down at him.

"You're a brat, do you know that?" he asked, lightly spanking my butt. I winked at him as I headed to my bedroom, dragging him with me. It had been way too long, and Donovan in his uniform was too much for me to control myself.

# CHAPTER FIFTEEN

I was going through all of my clothes, pulling out all of the items I wouldn't be wearing again for a while, like most of my shorts. I placed them all in a box and wrote on top what was inside. I hated packing, especially all alone. Donovan was working, so he couldn't help or even keep me company. I felt sorry for myself, and my growing tummy.

It was getting close to Thanksgiving and I wanted to be moved into Donovan's place in time to plan a Thanksgiving dinner there. I had invited Grandma and Shelly to spend the holiday with us. It was very exciting to be able to do the planning and the thought of cooking instead of poor Grandma doing it, was refreshing. Change was good, my therapist said. I had started to see him regularly again after leaving the hospital for the second time. The nightmares weren't there, as long as Donovan was beside me. However, the nights he was working, my demons waited for me.

A knock at the front door of my apartment caught my attention as I taped the last box of my summer clothes. That's odd, I thought. Anyone who knew me would call me before coming over. Maybe it was a salesman. I stood, walked to the front door, and looked out of the peephole. It was a police officer. My heart started pounding as dread chilled my body. I opened the door.

"May I help you, officer?" I asked, hoping he was at the wrong address. The last time an officer came to my door, I lost both my mother and father.

"Um… Yes… Miss Brady? Miss Angel Brady?" He fidgeted uncomfortably.

"Yes, that is me," I answered, though I wished I were anyone else at that moment.

"Miss Brady, I'm afraid I have some bad news. You are Donovan Mancini's emergency contact. Is that correct?" he cautiously asked.

"Yes," my voice croaked. "What's happened? Is he okay?" Every possible bad thing went through my mind.

"HHe was shot today, ma'am. He's stable, but we had to let you know, in case something happens. He's at St. Anne's Hospital." I felt my legs give as I crumbled to the floor.

Donovan was shot? No! He had to be okay. We were going to have a baby and finally everything was going smoothly. Normal. No drama, just boring, normal, everyday life. The officer grabbed me before I went completely down.

"Miss Brady? Are you okay? I can take you to him, if you'd like," he offered.

"Yes, please. How bad is it? Where was he shot? And by whom?" The questions just flew out of my mouth in my worry. He helped me up and I hastened over to get my purse and jacket.

"Ma'am, hold on, let me help you. He was shot in the chest area. I don't have many details, yet. I don't know his current condition. He was involved in a shoot-out with some guys at another human trafficking bust. That's all I can tell you right now. I'm sorry." He shared the limited details and held my elbow to walk down the stairs, to his patrol car.

The drive to the hospital was silent. I couldn't talk to the poor officer. He was only the bearer of bad news, but I found myself almost angry with him. I was angry with the police department for putting Donovan in danger. I was angry with Donovan for choosing a profession that could get him killed. Then, I wasn't angry anymore. I could not be mad at anyone, especially Donovan. He was only following his dream, saving people, getting the bad guys. He had to be okay. I couldn't live without him. I couldn't raise this baby without him. The baby needed his or her daddy. I found myself sobbing at the thought. No, this couldn't be. He had to pull through this. After everything we had been through already, I couldn't lose him now.

I was in a trance as we walked into the emergency department of the hospital. The officer spoke to the nurse at the counter, she stood and asked us to follow her. Walking behind her, I noticed we weren't going into the emergency room. We were headed to the Intensive Care Unit. My heart dropped. She stopped in front of a door and motioned for us to go inside. The officer, whose name I didn't even know, let me go in first.

There, in that hospital bed, lay Donovan. He had tubes coming out of his mouth, monitors hooked up to every part of his body, beeping loudly. He looked so small, so helpless. I was crushed.

"How is he? What damage has the bullet caused?" I asked the nurse as she moved to exit the room.

"The doctor will be right in to speak to you, Miss Brady," she stated and walked out, leaving me with my thoughts. The officer behind me cleared his throat.

"If you think you'll be okay here, I'm going to go back to the precinct. I'm so sorry for all of this, Miss Brady," he said. I turned to him.

"Of course. Thank you for bringing me, and it's not your

fault. I'm sorry if I was short with you earlier," I said quickly as he left the room.

I inched closer to the bed and sat on a chair.

"Oh, Donovan, what have you gotten yourself into? You need to pull through this," I whispered. There was a soft knock on the door. I turned to see who it was. A man with a white jacket stood there.

"Hello, Miss Brady is it?" he asked softly. It was the doctor, I assumed.

"Yes, I am Angel Brady," I replied. "Is he going to be okay? Please, tell me he's going to be okay," I said as tears spilled down my cheeks.

"Well, to be completely honest with you, the first twenty-four hours are the most critical. We had to perform emergency surgery to remove the bullet. We really won't know the extent of the damage until tomorrow. The bullet missed his heart, but it grazed the artery beside it. We were able to fix the artery, but he lost a massive amount of blood before he arrived. We gave him a few units of blood to replace what was lost." He waited for everything to sink in. I began to shake, violently. "Miss Brady? Angel, if I may, you have to calm down. It won't do him any good to wake up and have you in the bed next door," he said. He noted my protruding stomach. "It also isn't good for the baby."

"I know. I'm trying not to freak out right now," I said. I tried to calm myself, knowing what he said was the truth. I needed to be strong for Donovan right now, just as he had been strong for me so many times before. I looked at him again, with all of the tubes, and started sobbing again.

"Why does he have the tubes?" I asked the doctor.

"He just needs a little help breathing right now. If he wakes up, and can breathe on his own, we will be able to take them out," he explained. I nodded my understanding. "You should probably go back home and get some rest. If something changes, we will call you."

"I can't leave him, doctor. He is the reason I am alive today. I can't just leave him in this bed all alone," I whimpered. He watched me for a minute, and then nodded. He walked out of the room, said something to the nurses, and then came back in with one of them in tow. She had pillows and blankets in her hands.

"We will bring in a cot for you sleep on, Angel. We normally wouldn't allow visitors to stay in ICU, but I am going to go out on a limb and make an exception for Officer Donovan. Seeing how you look at him, I'm thinking it would do him a lot of good if you are here when he awakens."

I smiled my gratitude to him and the nurse as I took the bedding from her. The nurse smiled back to me. A minute later, a cot was indeed brought into the room, and placed in the corner of the room. I threw the bedding on top of it and walked back over to sit beside Donovan. It was painful to see him lying there, so vulnerable. He had always been my hero. I sniffled as the tears came again. I finally stood and walked to the cot and lay down.

I woke to the beeping sounds of Donovan's monitors going off. I jumped up and ran over to him. He was awake, but not happy. I hit the call button for the nurse. She burst into the room with needle in hand and gave him a shot in his IV. He calmed down a bit, staring at me. The nurse ran out of the room and then back in again, this time with the doctor.

"Well, Mr. Mancini, it appears you have decided to come back to us. Now, I want to try to take this tube out of your throat— but you have to work with me. Okay?" Donovan nodded to the doctor. His eyes met mine. I was freaking out. He winked at me. HE WINKED AT ME! My Donovan was still there!

The doctor instructed the nurse and Donovan on what to do to remove the tube. I walked out of the room, at that point, to keep from being sick. The emotional roller coaster the past twelve hours had me on, plus not eating or getting much sleep, had angered the baby.

After pacing the hallway for I don't know how long, the nurse finally came out.

"It's okay, Miss. You can go back in now. We're e finished. He won't be able to talk very well for a little bit, but I think he's going to be okay. He's asking for you," she said.

"Thank you." I stepped back into Donovan's room, his eyes found me immediately.

"Hey," I said softly as I came beside him.

"Hey," he whispered back. He acted like he was going to try to reach for me, but winced in pain. I sat on the edge of the bed, leaned over, and kissed him softly on the lips.

"You scared me, Officer Mancini," I whispered, as a tear slipped down my cheek.

"I'm so sorry," he tried to say, but started to cough. I reached over and grabbed the cup that was on the hospital tray. I held it up to his mouth so he could take a sip.

"Don't try to talk just yet, Donovan. You need your strength to get better," I chastised. He nodded his head, and kept quiet. I touched his cheek, just to prove to myself he was really there, alive.

"You just scared me, that's all. I never want to get a knock on the door like that again, got it?" I was rambling as I was straightening his sheets, trying to make him as comfortable as possible. Donovan nodded at me, and smiled a small smile. "I love you too much for you to be dying on me, mister."

"I love you, too, Angel," he croaked out.

"Shush...." I said. "Get some rest, babe. You're going to need it."

He closed his eyes and drifted off. I stood there for at least ten minutes, just watching him sleep. I was so thankful for another day with him. I couldn't believe my luck. He seemed as if he was going to pull through this, even if he had a long road to a full recovery.

Later that afternoon, the doctor came back in to check on Donovan. He grinned when he had seen we were half cuddled up on the bed. I jumped up as soon as I noticed he was in the room.

"No need to move on my behalf, Angel. I'm beginning to think you are better medicine than anything that I can give him," he chuckled and I blushed.

"How do you think he's healing?" I asked, hopefully.

"Well, he seems to be doing okay. His blood work came back a few minutes ago, and his hemoglobin is back to normal. That means he isn't bleeding internally any longer. His blood also does not show any signs of infection starting, so that is obviously good, too." I felt the weight of the world being lifted off of my shoulders at his words. Donovan was going to recover from this.

"However," the dreaded word nobody wanted to hear after good news, "he will need extensive physical therapy for his left arm. It seems he had some nerve damage when the bullet went through the back, before lodging in his shoulder." I sighed again, in relief.

"I think if physical therapy is the worst case scenario, then we are doing good here," I said. amd sat back down on the bed beside Donovan.

"I think you are right, Angel," Donovan agreed. I looked over at him and met his smile with my own. "As long as I can hold my baby when he or she is born, I'll be a happy man."

"I don't see that as being an issue, Mr. Mancini." The doctor stood at the foot of the bed scanning the charts. "I will be in to check on you again tomorrow. I don't think you need to be in ICU anymore, so I will write up an order to place you into a more comfortable room. Also, tomorrow, I want to take a look at that wound." He turned and left the room.

"Well, that was some much needed good news," I said as I settled in beside Donovan.

"Yes, it was. Now, I just have to convince him of letting me go home," Donovan agreed.

"Ha ha… Pretty sure you're going to be stuck here for a little while longer," I argued. "As much as I want you home, with me, I want you healthy even more." I kissed his head and stood up again. "I probably stink. I need to go home and take a shower. I'll be back as soon as I'm done."

"Okay, baby. I love you," he whispered, his eyes already closing for sleep..

"I love you back," I whispered and slipped out. I called Shelly to come to pick me up and take me back to my apartment. She was shocked, and a little upset I hadn't told her sooner what had happened to Donovan. After calmly explaining I was in shock myself, and I didn't want to concern anyone else unless I needed to, she decided to forgive me.

# CHAPTER SIXTEEN

After almost two weeks in the hospital, Donovan was going stir crazy. He was upset because Shelly and I had almost moved all of my things into his house. He wanted so badly to help, but they wouldn't let him escape the hospital. Now he knew how I felt. I swear, once they get you into these places, it is like pulling teeth to get them to let you leave.

On the day that he was finally released, I was trying to get everything ready for him at home. I wanted everything easily accessible for him. I reached up, above my head to grab some coffee cups, and a piece of paper fell to the ground. I bent to pick it up, and found it was a photo. It was a black and white of a couple holding a small boy. I turned it over and read the handwriting: Donovan, 4 years old. It must have been his parents who were holding him. They all looked so happy in the picture. My heart hurt for that little boy who was forced to grow up too soon a few years after this photo was taken. I was putting the picture on the refrigerator door when my phone rang. I looked down, it was Donovan. He must be ready to go, I thought.

"Hey, babe," I answered immediately.

"Hey, yourself. I actually got a ride, so you can relax a little bit longer. You don't have to come to pick me up," he stated. It sounded odd to me, but I didn't question him.

"Okay. As long as you're sure you have someone to be there for you when they finally let you leave."

"Oh, no worries. I'm not alone. Actually, babe, I won't be home right away. I have to go to the station and fill out some incident forms. I shouldn't be too long, but I wanted to let you know so you didn't worry." I wasn't sure why he felt he had to explain himself to me. "Anyway, I'll see you soon, okay? I love you."

"Okay. I love you, too," I said as we both ended the call.

A few hours later, he was letting himself into the house. I was so excited to see him that I almost jumped on him when he walked in. He was such a sight for sore eyes. I walked with him to the couch, so he could sit down. Not knowing what he did the rest of the afternoon, I just sat and waited for him to start talking.

"So, another human trafficking ring, huh?" I asked abruptly. He looked at me, confused. I watched as understanding reached his face. "Did you at least get a big bad guy, this time?"

"Yes, Angel. We got the lead guy. He is actually the person who shot me. He came at me, and I pulled the trigger. We must have started shooting at the same time." I shuddered as the thought of death ran across my mind, once again. Guns. Sometimes I think they shouldn't exist because of all of the lives they've taken. At the same time, they have also saved my life, my grandma's life, and now, Donovan's.

"Good," I said and left the conversation at that. I didn't want to talk about it any longer. It was bad enough I almost lost Donovan.

"So," he began as he looked around his house, "What have you been up to? I can see you've been busy."

"Oh, you know, just unpacking and adding my touch to this man cave," I said as I wrapped my arms around his neck.

"I'm glad. I want you to feel comfortable, and to make yourself at home here, Angel. This is your house, too, now." He pulled me close in for a deep, passionate kiss. Oh, how I'd missed this closeness.

"As long as you are here with me, I'll always feel like I'm home. I love you so much, Donovan," I said as I leaned in to kiss him again. I pulled back. "We had better stop this or I'll never get around to cooking your dinner." I laughed as I stood up and walked to the kitchen. The landline started ringing, so I walked into the living room to answer it. Donovan had an angry look on his face.

"Just let it ring, Angel. It's nobody important."

"Okay," I said, feeling a very odd vibe coming from him. I wondered who it was, but I didn't want to be too nosy. I went back to my task in the kitchen, starting the spaghetti for dinner. The phone rang again, and I heard Donovan answer it. I tried not to hear what he was saying, but I couldn't help my curiosity.

"What do you want," he said quietly. "I thought I told you not to call me anymore... I'm fine...I don't care what is going on with you... and you shouldn't be worrying about me. We're through... How did you even find out?" He was silent for a bit. "Look, I don't know what it is with you, but I told you we were done months ago... Whatever... I'll believe it when I see it." He slammed the phone on the hook.

"Everything okay, babe?" I asked as I joined him in the living room.

"Yes, everything is fine," he answered shortly. I didn't like this side of Donovan. He was almost scary. He could see I was getting uncomfortable, he changed his tone. "I'm sorry, Angel. That was this chick I was seeing a while back. I ended it months ago, but she just won't give up."

"It's odd, don't you think, that a cop would have a stalker?" I was almost amused at the thought. That is, until I looked in his eyes again. He was actually looking a little nervous. "Well, she'll stop soon. Just let me answer next time." He laughed at that.

"She's crazy. I mean, she was a little odd when we were dating, but since we broke up, she's just nuts," he said, shaking his head.

"Yeah, well, I'm crazier. You know, hormones and all," I said as I winked at him. The phone started ringing again. I moved to go answer, but he stopped me.

"Ignore it," he said, "Eventually, she'll get the hint."

"Fine," I sighed, and went into the kitchen to put the garlic bread in the oven. "Dinner will be done in about twenty minutes."

"Okay. I'm going to go hop in the shower real quick. I have to get this hospital smell off of me," he called to me. I heard him get up and walk into the bathroom. As I was draining the spaghetti noodles, the phone rang once again. That's it. I'm done playing games. I walked into the living room, picked up the phone, and walked back to the kitchen.

"Hello?" I said.

"Um… Hello… Who is this? Is Donovan available?" the confused voice asked.

"Actually, he's in the shower. I am Angel. Is there something I can help you with?" I asked. I heard a snicker.

"Angel… How fitting." As she spoke, I began to feel my face heat up with anger. "Well, 'Angel', my name is Kameryn. I am Donovan's girlfriend," she said with a cocky tone.

"Oh, really? Well, 'Kameryn', you see, the thing is, I know who you are. It's funny you say you are Donovan's girlfriend when I, in fact, live with him." I could not help the smile that came across my face as I heard her gasp.

"How could he do this to me?" she started sobbing. "We're going to have a baby!" I almost dropped the phone when I heard those words. Donovan knocked her up? He failed to mention that to me, I thought, as I started to shake.

"You're pregnant?" I whispered. "How far along?"

She hesitated before answering.

"Well, I'm not sure, exactly," she stammered. "I haven't been to the doctor, yet, but I would say around three months." Her voice lightened as she realized what effect hearing that news had on me.

"Three months, and you haven't been to a doctor, yet?" I asked.

"I don't have insurance. Donovan said he would take care of it all," she said. I felt like someone had just kicked me in the stomach.

"Okay, well," I started, "I'll let him know you called, and have him call you back as soon as he's done." I hung up on her. As much as I hated when people did that to me, I just couldn't handle hearing her voice any longer. In a trance, I went through the motions of pulling the garlic bread out of the oven and setting the table. I heard the bathroom door open as Donovan stepped out.

"It smells amazing out here," he said and walked into the kitchen. He pulled a chair out at the table and sat down. I turned around, looked at him, but said nothing. I looked away, and started plating up the food. I handed him his plate, and sat down with my own. I felt him looking at me, but I couldn't bring myself to look up from my plate. I played with the noodles for a few moments. Finally, I looked at him. He was questioning me with his eyes. I still said nothing.

"What's up, Angel?" he asked. "Why are you so quiet?" I could feel my throat start to burn as the tears threatened to come. I shook my head and stared at my dinner. I couldn't eat it, my appetite was gone. Just then, I felt a little flutter in my stomach. It was the baby moving. I remembered the doctor telling me it would feel like a little butterfly when he or she would move. I couldn't help the tears at that moment. They were already sliding down my cheeks. Donovan jumped up, and hurried to my side.

"What's wrong? Did something happen while I was in the shower?" He looked down to where my hand rested on my belly. "Is there something wrong with the baby? Do we need to go to the hospital? Talk to me, Angel!" He was yelling now, which only made me cry harder.

"I spoke to Kameryn, Donovan," I said, waiting for him to understand. I wanted to hear he had gotten her pregnant out of his mouth. He cursed, stood up, and walked over to the counter before leaning against it. He glanced at the floor, and shook his head before turning back to me.

"You should've just let it ring, Angel," he said. The tears stopped, and the anger took their place.

"Why? Do you honestly think that just because you ignore her, she'll go away? She's having your baby, Donovan! Which, by the way, you didn't tell me. Why didn't you tell me? Don't you think that is something I should know?" Now it was my turn to get loud.

"What?! Did she tell you that? Oh my God..." He walked over to where I sat and knelt down beside me. "She's not pregnant, Angel." He must have seen the doubt in my eyes, because he rushed to explain. "We haven't slept together in over five months. Even when we did, I used protection. If she's knocked up, there's no way in hell that baby's mine." He laid his head down on my lap. I unconsciously ran my hand through his dark hair. I wanted so badly to believe him, but in the back of my mind, I could not understand why Kameryn would tell me that, if it weren't true. The words of our conversation jolted me.

"She said she was three months pregnant. I'm four months. That means we would have been together when she got pregnant," I whispered, more to myself than to Donovan.

"I swear on everything I have, I didn't have sex with her three months ago, babe. I broke it off with her long before that. I would never cheat on you. I knew the moment I laid eyes on you, you were the one for me." He looked up at me, and I saw fear in his eyes. It was similar to the same look I had seen when I woke up in the hospital.

I took a deep breath. "I just don't understand why she would say something like that to me. She said she was your girlfriend, and when I told her that I was living here, she flipped out. She said you two were going to have a baby. I asked her how far along she was, and she told me she hadn't even been to the doctor yet. Who doesn't go to the doctor for three months when she's pregnant?" I was rambling, half to myself, and half to Donovan. I was trying to make sense of everything that had taken place in the past hour.

Donovan squeezed my hands. "I told you, she's crazy, Angel. She told me a while back she was pregnant, and it was supposedly mine. I told her there was no way she was pregnant with my kid. She's either lying about even being pregnant, or she got knocked up long after I broke it off with her." He put both of his hands on my cheeks, and made me look at him. "I'm telling you, Ang, this is not my baby, that is, if she is even carrying one."

I stood, picked up my plate, and scraped it off into the trash. I placed the dirty dish into the dishwasher and considered the phone call again. Kameryn did sound very suspicious when I asked her about how far along she was. It was as if she was trying to think of something to say. I remembered how happy she sounded as I was getting upset. It hit me. That bitch! She knew exactly what she was doing. I turned and looked at Donovan, who was waiting silently for me to say something. I walked over, stood beside him, and he wrapped his arms around my waist. He pressed his cheek against my belly as he held me close.

"I'm so sorry you were put in the middle of this, babe," he sniffled as he looked up at me. My heart ached as I wiped the tears from his cheek.

"I believe you," I said.

His eyes shot to mine. "You do?"

"Yes, Donovan. I mean, yes, I was in shock at first, then angry, and finally, hurt. But, now that I think about all of it, none of it makes sense. I think she was lying to me. You have never given me a reason to question my trust in you. You have done everything to make me happy. You say you love me, and I believe you," I said as I kissed his forehead. He let out the breath that he must have been holding, with a long whistle.

"God, do I ever love you. You are my world, my everything. And…" He bent down to kiss my belly. "You're going to have MY baby." I laughed at his emphasis on the word 'my.'.

"I love you, too. I'm sorry I even doubted you," I apologized.

"Don't be sorry. I don't even know how I'd act if some guy called and told me that you were his girlfriend," he growled. "Let alone the baby you were carrying was his." He visibly shuddered at the words. I smiled.

"Well, now that dinner has been ruined, I'm thinking we should eat a big tub of ice cream and watch a movie." I grabbed his plate and repeated the steps that I did with my own.

"The spaghetti was good, babe. Thank you for cooking. I'm sorry she ruined it."

"Don't worry about it. I'm over it. Just wait until she calls again…" I threatened. He laughed, loudly.

"I'd actually like to be in the room to witness that phone call," he said after he caught his breath. " A movie and ice cream sounds great. What are we watching? Chick flick or Horror?"

"Definitely horror," I said as I grabbed the chocolate ice cream out of the freezer, along with two spoons, and walked past him into the living room. A horror movie just seemed too fitting at the time. I was feeling pretty murderous myself. I didn't want anything sappy because then I would probably cry. I'd cried enough for one day. For a lifetime, actually.

# CHAPTER SEVENTEEN

Thanksgiving was a success. I had somehow managed to cook a turkey, without burning it, and made the stuffing just how my grandma taught me to. This all surprised me. Shelly brought a 'friend' along with her, and to my utter surprise, so did my grandma.

Apparently, Grandma had met this man, David, at one of her bingo gatherings. He was seventy-five years old, and a ballroom dance instructor. My grandma seemed smitten by him, and I couldn't have been happier for her. As for Shelly, her new boyfriend's name was Cory. They met while she was in Florida. I was actually surprised they had lasted this long. I decided to tell Shelly just that when we were alone, maybe while cleaning everything up.

"Well, you see, he's actually a really good guy." Shell paused. "Plus, he's amazing in bed," she added, giggling.

"I didn't need to know all of that," I replied, shaking my head, smiling. Shelly was never one to beat around the bush. She was honest, even if a bit callous. I finished drying and put the last dish away and turned toward her. "Anyway, he's obviously doing something right, to be able to keep your attention for this long. If he makes you happy, then I'm happy for you, Shell."

"He does make me happy," she murmured, thoughtfully, almost as if the statement surprised her as well. She grabbed my hands, and looked me in the eyes. "There's something else, Ang."

"Okay? And what might that be?" I asked, my curiosity growing.

"I may or may not be a couple of weeks late…" She waited for me to realize what she was saying.

"Late? For what?" I asked. Then it hit me. "Oh!!! What?! Are you serious?" She nodded, smiling.

"I don't know for sure, but I'm scared shitless. I don't know anything about being a mom, honestly, and I can't drink." She was whining. I had to laugh. "What's so funny?"

"First of all, you having a baby could be the best thing ever happened to you. Maybe you'll settle down a little." I dodged the punch headed for my shoulder. "Second, we would be having babies very close to each other. Six months ago, I would have laughed at anyone who would have said this would be happening to either of us."

"I know, right?!" Shelly agreed. "I'm so nervous. Cory is excited, which is starting to wear off on me. I haven't even had the guts to take a test yet."

"We can go pick one up tomorrow morning, if you want. The stores aren't open now," I offered.

"Sounds good. I would like it if you were there with me when I find out. Thank you," she said and hugged me.

We ended the conversation as Grandma walked into the kitchen. She was glowing. It really warmed my heart to see her so happy. David was a couple of years older than her, but she didn't care. She decided that, much like Shelly, that I needed to know that David was like a stallion in bed. The very last thing I wanted a picture of in my mind, was that of my grandma doing the dirty.

"Hey, girls," she sang as she sashayed her way over to us. She hugged me, and kissed my cheek. "David and I are going to head home. Thank you so much for dinner, Angel. It was very good. You made me a proud grandma today."

"I learned everything from the best. Thank you for coming, Grandma," I said as I hugged her back. "Call me when you get home. It's starting to snow again."

"I will, honey." David walked in the room and put his hand out for me to shake.

"It was very nice to meet you, David. You're welcome here any time," I said, stepped in closer, hugged him and kissed his cheek. Then I whispered so only he could hear me, "You make her so happy. Happier than I've ever seen her. Thank you for that." He smiled and kissed me on the forehead.

"I'm the lucky one in this relationship, sweetie. She keeps me young." He winked and looked past me, to Grandma. They both were beaming. I thought my heart would burst with the love. "Thank you for having us, Angel."

"You bet," I said. "Come again, please."

We said our goodbyes and they were off to head home. I was sad to see Grandma leave, but at the same time, I was ready to change into some pajamas and cuddle up with Donovan on the couch. Shelly and Cory, staying with us for the holiday, headed off to bed, leaving us alone for the first time all day. Donovan walked up behind me, and wrapped his arms around my growing waist.

"I'm going to have to say that Thanksgiving was a huge success," he murmured in my ear, giving me goose bumps. I leaned my head to side so that he could kiss my neck.

"Yes, Mr. Mancini, I would say so as well. I can't believe my grandma found a new love interest," I said, laughing. "She seems so happy." Donovan joined me in the laughter.

"She sure does." He rocked me while we remained in a locked embrace.

"I'm glad. She deserves it. All of the years following the death of my parents, she invested all of her energy in raising me. She never went on dates, never even had a girls' night out. All of her attention was given to me," I said, guiltily.

"And she loved every minute of it. She just needed to meet the right man, at the right time. It just so happens the time wasn't until recently," Donovan said. He had a way with words, getting rid of my worries and guilt immediately. I didn't think I could love this man any more than I did at that moment.

"Thank you," I said.

"For what?" he asked, confused.

"Everything. Just for being you."

"Well, then," he laughed. "You're welcome. I guess you just bring out the best of me."

He took my hand and led me to the bathroom. He turned the water on and started to fill the tub. He reached into the cabinet, pulling out some bath salts and poured them in the water. I looked at him questioningly, and he just shook his head as he undressed me. He then took his own clothes off, stepped into the tub, and reached for me. I gave him my hand and we both sat slowly into the warm water. It felt amazing. Donovan massaged my shoulder and upper back, effectively relaxing my sore muscles. I leaned back against him, relaxing the rest of my body. I was almost asleep when all of a sudden, I felt a little 'thump' in my stomach. It made me jump which scared Donovan.

"Are you okay, babe?" he asked as I sat straight up.

"Yeah… I think the baby just kicked me. Actually, I'm almost positive. I don't know what else that could have been," I laughed, in awe. Donovan's hand immediately went to my stomach.

"Really? That's awesome! I wonder if I can feel it. Think he will do it again?" he asked. I grabbed his hand and put it where I felt the kick. We waited for a few, and nothing happened. I was beginning to think I was feeling things, when it happened again. Donovan jumped this time.

"I felt it! I felt him kick!" he exclaimed. "Wow. That was just amazing. There really is a little person in there." I had to laugh at his excitement, adding to my own.

"Well... Yeah..." I said. I started to get up out of the tub to dry off. "So, you think it's a boy, huh?"

"Why do you say that?" he asked.

"You kept saying 'he and him'."

"Did I? Must be wishful thinking."

"You want a boy?" I asked.

"I would like a boy, but I will be happy with whatever, as long as he or she is healthy," he answered, honestly.

"Me, too," I said. I finished drying off and put my robe on. It barely tied in the front these days. Looks like I'll need to go shopping soon. I sighed. Donovan was watching me with amusement, and there was something a little mischievous in his eyes. "What?" I asked.

"You are so beautiful," he said, making me blush. I didn't think I would ever get tired of him saying that to me.

"Thank you."

"It's true. I've always thought so. Now that you're pregnant, though, it's like you have this glow about you." He paused. "You know, like you have a light inside of you." He stepped out of the tub and grabbed a towel.

"I do have a light inside of me," I said and turned toward him. He was smiling.

"I want to put something else inside of you," he hinted. I felt my cheeks warm up as I walked out of the bathroom to our bedroom. He followed right behind me, wearing nothing but the towel.

As we kissed, I heard my cell phone ring. Grunting, I got up and ran downstairs to the living room. It was Grandma telling me

she and David had made it home. I thanked her for calling and
went back to Donovan. He was waiting for me, attempting to be
patient. Our love making session didn't take as long as it usually
did, but I was alright with it. Whoever said sex isn't the same
during pregnancy was correct. It was almost better. Everything
was more sensitive, which is why it didn't last as long. It didn't
take long to send me over the edge, effectively wearing me out. It
wasn't very long after, I passed out in his arms.

I awakened to a sound from downstairs. I lifted my head and
waited, trying to figure out if what I heard was in fact real, or if it
was part of a dream. I heard the noise again. I shook Donovan's
shoulder. He awoke, startled.

"What is it? What's wrong?" he whispered, concerned.

"I keep hearing something downstairs." I didn't get the words
out my mouth before he jumped up out of bed and threw on a
pair of jeans.

"Stay in bed, babe. I'll go see," he whispered. Yeah, right, like
I was going to let him go down there alone. I wasn't taking any
chances of him getting hurt again. I stood, put my pajamas on,
and attempted to wrap my robe around me. I tiptoed to the top
of the steps and listened. I heard Donovan speak.

"What the fuck do you think you're doing here, Kameryn?"

Did I hear him right? Was Kameryn in our home on
Thanksgiving night? What in the hell was wrong with this
woman? I quietly walked down the stairs, peeking around the
corner so I could see them. Donovan had turned the living room
light on, so it made it easy to see them both.

"I had to come and see you, Donovan. I miss you," Kameryn
said as she reached her arms around his neck, trying to kiss him.
I felt my anger grow to the point of explosion. She had short
blonde hair, was around the same height and weight as me, and
was wearing a black mini skirt, and a halter top that was barely

keeping her breasts inside it. Did someone forget to tell her it was winter out?

Donovan grabbed her hands off of his neck, and took a step back. She tried to come to him again, but he stopped her with his hands. I watched him wince, as his shoulder must have been still sore. He had only been to three sessions with the physical therapist for it.

"Are you fucking crazy? You can't be here. You can't be anywhere near me. Go home, Kameryn, before I call the police. My girl is upstairs, and if you upset her, you're really going to have a cat by the tail. I'm warning you."

"You're girl? Who? Angel? No way… I thought I scared that dumb bitch off. I told her we were going to have a baby." She was actually laughing. That was all it took for me. I stepped into the room just as Donovan turned to grab his cell phone from the coffee table. Our eyes met. He gave me a pleading look. I shook my head.

"Is there some reason why you thought you needed to be here in the middle of the night, on Thanksgiving, Kameryn?" I asked, stepping closer to her. She looked me up and down, stopping at my belly. Her face flushed with rage.

"You're pregnant?!" she screamed and looked from me, to Donovan, then back to me. "Couldn't you take a hint, bitch? Donovan's mine! We're going to have a family." She put her hand on her very flat stomach. I laughed. Being pregnant, my sense of smell was well enhanced. I could smell the alcohol on her from six feet away. "You think this is funny, bitch?" She stepped toward me. Donovan quickly stopped her from getting any closer.

"I think you have lost your mind, lady." I looked past Donovan at her. She glared back at me.

"Kameryn, this is your last warning. Leave. Now. Or I am calling the cops," Donovan warned.

"I'm not leaving until you tell her that I'm pregnant with your baby!" she spat. I looked again at her flat belly.

"Okay, this is ridiculous," I said. "I know you're not pregnant, Kameryn."

"What the fuck do you think you know?"

"Well, the fact you would be showing, at least a little bit, by now," I started. "Not to mention I can smell the liquor on you from here. If you are pregnant, then you need to be locked up for that alone."

Kameryn looked, once again, at Donovan, before jumping around him and lunging at me. Donovan tried to grab her, but missed. She almost got me when Shelly appeared out of nowhere, tackling her to the ground. Kameryn landed under her, with a loud grunt.

"Get off of me!" she screamed at Shelly. Kameryn turned her attention back to me. "I would have been pregnant if you hadn't come into the picture. You ruined my life, you bitch!"

"Fuck you! You were seriously about to attack a pregnant woman. What is wrong with you?" Shelly screamed back as she punched Kameryn in the face. Kameryn squirmed her way out of the hold Shelly had on her, stood up quickly, and kicked Shelly in the stomach. Shelly coughed, then cursed, curling into a ball to the floor. Cory chose that moment to step into the room, grabbing Kameryn in a bear hug. Donovan was dialing his cell as I ran over to my best friend, who just saved me and my baby.

"Shelly? Are you okay?" I cried. I put my hand on her shoulder, pulling her over to me. I looked down, and there was blood on the floor. "Oh my God! Donovan!" I screamed. He came over to see what I was screaming about.

"Send an ambulance, too," he said into his phone and ended the call. He glared at Kameryn. "I hope this was all worth it, Kameryn."

"What are you talking about?" she spat out, trying to break free from Cory's hold. Donovan walked over to them, with his handcuffs in his hand and relieved Cory. He cuffed a very pissed off Kameryn to the chair while Cory rushed over to a crying Shelly.

"Shelly, I'm so sorry," I whispered.

"It's not your fault, Ang. That bitch is lucky she got a cheap shot in or I'd have beat her ass," she grunted in pain. a She glared at Kameryn.

The police showed up first, taking Kameryn away. The ambulance wasn't too far behind, thankfully. They put Shelly on the gurney, and loaded her into the vehicle. Cory rode with them. Donovan and I followed them to the hospital.

When we arrived, they rushed Shelly into the trauma room. Cory went with her, while Donovan and I stayed in the waiting room. We sat there for an hour, until Cory finally came out. I had my head on Donovan's shoulder when I saw him. I jumped up and ran to meet him. He looked so exhausted. The normally, tall, muscular, tan, man looked pale and very frail. My heart fell.

"What's happening? Is Shelly okay? What are they doing for her?" I bombarded him with questions.

"She lost the baby. She was pregnant, afterall," he said. "The blow caused her to miscarry." The tears flowed.

"Oh, Cory, I'm so sorry," I whispered, tears falling down my cheeks as well. "Can I see her?"

"Yeah. She's down the hall, last room on the left."

I looked at Donovan, who nodded to me, and I walked away to my best friend. I approached the room with the guilt of everything happening tonight washing over me. Shelly had lost her baby while protecting me. I peeked into the room. Shelly was lying there, her back to the door, curled up. I stepped inside and closed the door behind me. She looked over her shoulder at me as I neared her.

"Hey," she said quietly.

"Hey," I whispered. "Cory told me. I don't know what to say, Shell. I'm so, so sorry." I was sobbing now.

"Hey, now, stop, Ang." She was crying, too. "This is not your fault. That woman was crazy. She was going to attack you."

"I know, but you stopped her, and look what has happened. Look at what protecting me has caused."

"I'd do it again, Angel," she said softly. "She will get hers." Her words and tone turned cold. I felt the same way.

"Yes, she sure will," I agreed. A soft knock at the door interrupted us. I went to open it. An officer stood with Donovan. Shelly looked past me and nodded that she was ready to talk to the police. I let them in.

"Hey, Shelly. How are you feeling? Are you sure you're up for this?" Donovan asked, softly.

"Yes. Let's get this over with. The sooner we do, the sooner that lunatic will be off the streets for good."

"Okay. This is Officer Brown. He is going to be asking most of the questions. He knows what happened with my statement, along with Angel's and Cory's. He just needs to get yours. He will be really quick, okay?" Donovan pulled up a chair. I sat over beside Shelly, and held her hand. She smiled gratefully at me and squeezed.

After she finished her statement, we discovered Kameryn would be charged with manslaughter, because of the loss of Shelly's baby. That made it a little bit easier on Shelly, and me too, for that matter. It was nice knowing she wouldn't get away with this, and she was facing a lot of time behind bars. I sat with Shelly for a couple more hours before finally telling her she needed rest and I would be back the next day. I hugged Cory, and apologized once more. He told me the same thing Shelly did, but I just could not get rid of the feeling I was partially to blame for this.

When Donovan and I arrived at our house, I sat on the couch and broke down. I cried for Shelly, I cried for Cory, I cried for their baby, and I cried for myself. Donovan came to me, sat, and gathered me in his arms.

"Shh, Angel. It'll be okay," he soothed.

"Shelly lost her baby because she was protecting me, Donovan," I wailed. "She should never have jumped in like that."

"Angel, if you didn't know for sure you were pregnant, and Shelly was in danger, would you just stand by and watch someone attack her?" he asked.

"Of course not," I admitted.

"She was standing up for her pregnant best friend."

"I know. I would have done the same. It's just so sad." I sighed.

"It is, I agree. But if anyone is to blame for all of this, it should be me," he said.

"You? Why?"

"I should have gotten a restraining order against her when I realized she wasn't going to go away. After I broke it off with her, I guess I was just hoping she would stop."

"A restraining order is just a piece of paper, Donovan. She would have still come over here. She is crazy, and I'm sure no law would have kept her away from you."

"I guess," he said, regretfully. "Oh, I forgot to tell you— Kameryn was lying about the baby. She was never pregnant. Not with my child, or anyone else's. Anyway, you need to get some sleep. Our baby is going to think you're upset with him. Or her…" He stood, pulling me up with him.

"I knew it," I said as he led me to the bedroom. We went to bed, and I had a new nightmare that night.

This one was of a baby crying, but I couldn't find it, no matter how hard I tried. It was just wailing away and was nowhere in sight. Suddenly, Kameryn appeared. She was standing on a edge of a cliff. As I neared her, I saw she was laughing hysterically, holding a baby by its arm, dangling it over the edge. I watched in horror when she let go of it, and it fell to its demise.

I awoke suddenly, my breathing heavy, heart pounding. I put my hand on my stomach, reminding myself my baby was still in there. As if he or she knew I needed it at that moment, I received a nice little kick. That calmed me enough to try to go back to sleep. It was difficult. I went back to thinking about Shelly, and how I was never going to be able to make up for what she had lost for me. This was one Thanksgiving that started out perfect, but quickly turned into one that wanted to forget.

# CHAPTER EIGHTEEN

Shelly only spent one night in the hospital. She was allowed to come home the next afternoon. When I arrived to check on her, she was like a completely different person. It was both relieving, and scary, at the same time. She asked Cory to go on home and called me to come pick her up. I walked into her room, she was dressed and ready to go, sitting in a chair beside the window. I knocked on the door, and she turned to me, smiling.

"Hey, lady," she said.

"Hey, honey. How are you feeling?" I asked.

"I'm good. They said the pain should go away after a couple of days," she began and then her smile grew wider. "They also said just because I lost this baby, it doesn't mean I will have any problems with getting pregnant again in the future." I sighed and walked over to kneel down beside her.

"That's great news, Shell."

"I know! I told Cory we can try again when the time is right." I almost fell over on the floor after that statement. Shelly was actually serious about this guy. She was planning a future with him.

"You really like this guy, huh?" I asked.

"I do. He stayed with me here, at the hospital, all night. Every

142

time I woke up, he was sitting there, right beside me." She smiled again. "I think I'm falling in love with him. He told me last night he wants to marry me."

"I'm really happy to hear that, Shelly," I started, "but please, be sure this is something you really want before you make any rash decisions."

"Oh, don't you worry your pretty little head," she said. "I never planned to get married in the first place. It's crazy for me to even think about." She laughed. I laughed, too.

"You do whatever it takes to make you happy. You deserve it," I said, tears building in my eyes. Stupid hormones, I thought, get a hold of yourself, Angel.

Shelly stood abruptly and walked over to the window. She stared out for a couple of minutes, and I was beginning to worry about her again. She turned toward me and I could see the tears streaming down her face. I walked over to hug her. She hugged me back, tightly.

"I'm so sorry this has all happened to you, Shell," I whispered. She pulled back and looked me deep in the eyes.

"Stop apologizing like it was your fault, Angel. You had no clue as to what that crazy lady was going to do. She was coming after you, even though she knew you were pregnant. When I came into the living room to see what all the noise was about, I saw the look in her eyes. It was murderous. She wasn't going to let Donovan go without one hell of a fight. When she came at you, I saw red and pounced," she explained.

As the events of the night before played through my head, I became very angry with Kameryn. I wanted to strangle her myself after I thought about it in more detail. Shelly was right, she was nuts. She would have had no problems at all hurting me, or the child I was carrying. Thinking about this did nothing but anger me even more at the fact she made Shelly lose her baby.

"Well, are you ready to break me out of this joint?" Shelly asked, back to her normal self again. I was really beginning to worry about how she was handling this whole situation. I was hoping she wouldn't break down hard in the future. I didn't want to see her hit a depression too low for me to help her out of it. It wasn't in her nature, but this was a whole new story.

"Yes, ma'am. Let's get out of here," I said and picked up her paperwork.

The drive back to my place was quiet, Shelly and I both lost in our own thoughts. I glanced over at her every now and then, just to be sure that she was alright. When we pulled into my drive, I noticed Cory's car in front of the house. This made me smile inside. He really seemed to care about Shelly, and she needed that right now.

We walked inside, and Donovan met us in the kitchen. He reached out and grabbed Shelly in a big hug. He showed her a chocolate cake he had made while we were gone. He didn't say a word as he took out four plates, forks, and served it to all of us. We all ate in silence, enjoying the moistness of the cake. Shelly was the first, as always, to break that silence.

"Wow, Donovan, this is amazing," she said. She turned to me. "You better keep a hold of this one, Angel, or I may steal him, just to cook for me." She laughed at herself, which made all of us laugh as well. That broke the tension building up since the night before.

"Yeah, I guess I'll keep him around for a while." I smirked at his indignant face. I leaned over and kissed him, showing him he wasn't going anywhere, anytime soon.

"Don't let her kid you," Donovan said. "She couldn't live without me. Or my cooking." That got another round of laughs. I looked at Shelly, feeling much better, thinking this was a good sign that things would, eventually, go back to normal.

Shelly and Cory hung around for a few more hours before

they went home. Shelly promised to call me and let me know they made it. Once they were gone, I went over and slumped down on the couch. The baby kicked as soon as I got comfortable. I reached down and rubbed my belly.

"It's okay, little one. Everything will be okay. You are my pride and joy, and you have a lot of people who care about, and are going to protect, you." I told him or her.

"I wonder if babies can actually hear when people are talking to them," Donovan said from the doorway, making me jump.

"I have always heard they can, but I'm not sure." I laughed.

"When is your next ultrasound. Will they be able to tell what we're having?" he asked.

"It's in a couple of weeks, and yes. Do we really want to know?"

"I don't know. I guess I would like to know. This waiting to find out is for the birds." His excitement was contagious. I wanted to find out the sex of the baby, too.

"Okay. We will find out a couple of weeks, then."

Donovan sat down beside me and pulled me over and on to his lap. He laid his hands on my belly, and the baby must have known, because he kicked. I thought Donovan was going to jump up and throw me on the floor.

"That was awesome! I think we have a future football player on our hands." He giggled.

"Maybe. Or a future ballerina." I was grinning now. We argued the pro and con of having a boy or a girl. Finally, I decided to change the subject. "Do you think Shelly is going to be okay?"

"Oh, I think she will be. She has Cory, and we are only five minutes away."

"Yeah." I hesitated. "I hope you're right. At first, it was as if she wasn't even going to mourn the loss. I mean, I understand she was only a few weeks along, but..."

"Babe, people handle these things differently. Some become

so depressed they can't leave their beds, and some get over it really fast. It looks like Shelly is one to get over things pretty quickly. A lot like you, actually." He buried his face in my neck. The baby kicked again, and I swear, it did a summersault at that moment. It was as if he or she was saying, 'Hey! No friskiness, mister dad.' I laughed as I stood, a little wobbly, then yawned.

"I hope you're right, Donovan," I said. I felt everyone should mourn, even if it was for a baby only a few weeks into pregnancy.

"Me too," he replied quietly. He stood as well, and took my hand in his. "Well, it looks like it's bed time for you, young lady."

I heard my cell phone ring as I walked into the bedroom. I walked back down to the living room and grabbed the phone off of the coffee table. It was Cory. Frowning, I answered.

"Hey, Cory. What's up?" I asked, cautiously. He was silent for a few seconds. "Cory?" I said, again.

"Um, hey, Angel. I'm sorry for calling so late, but I haven't seen Shelly in a few hours now." His voice was full of concern. My heart dropped to the floor.

"Where are you?" I asked.

"I'm at my place. She asked to be alone so I left. I told her I'd call her in a while to check on her. I don't know what to do. I guess I was hoping you had heard from her. I don't want to go barging into her place. That would just piss her off," he said, and he was right. If Shelly asked for her space, you gave it to her. "Like I said, I just don't know what to do." As he spoke, I returned to the bedroom to get Donovan. He would know what to do.

"Okay, Cory. It's okay. I'm sure she's fine. I will go and check on her," I said. Donovan perked up at my words.

"Alright. Thanks, Angel. Will you call me?" Cory asked.

"Of course," I saidthen hung up.

"What's going on?" Donovan asked as I was putting my shoes back on.

"That was Cory. I guess Shelly asked to be alone earlier when she got home and he hasn't been able to reach her on the phone since. I'm going to go over to her place and check on her," I answered. I stood and put my coat on, grabbing my purse and keys. Donovan acted as if he were going to get out of bed and put his shoes on, too.

"Want me to tag along?"

"No, thanks. I'll go alone. I don't know what state of mind she's in, or if she will even want to see me. She's not answering Cory's phone calls, so I'm assuming she isn't wanting male company," I said. I was to the door, then turned around to say, "I love you," and left.

I pulled up in front of Shelly's place, and noticed her lights were on inside. I got out of my car and walked up to her door. I knocked and waited. No answer. I knocked again. Nothing.

"Shelly?" I yelled. I put my ear to the door to listen, hoping for something, even the slightest of sounds, to let me know she was okay. I heard nothing. I checked the doorknob. The door was unlocked. I slowly opened it and peeked inside. I couldn't see anyone in the living room. I tip-toed toward the kitchen. She wasn't in there, either.

"Shelly?" I called again, and again. I received no reply. My heart started to beat faster with the familiar feeling of dread. Where was she? I continued on my trek, walking from room to room. I got to the bathroom. I could hear water running. The door was closed, but there was a light on. I knocked on the door.

"Shelly, honey it's Angel. Are you okay?" I asked and waited. Nothing. I heard sniffling and my heart leapt. I turned the handle and slowly opened the door. I saw her. Shelly was sitting in the bathtub, fully clothed. The water was overflowing onto the floor. I stepped through the puddling water, shut the water off, and grabbed a towel.

"What's going on, honey?" I asked as I pulled the drain plug, letting the water out of the tub. She didn't say anything to me. She just looked at me, or more like, through me. Shelly had left the building. There was nothing there but the shell of her. She said nothing as I pulled her to her feet, and wrapped the towel around her. She just stood there, staring ahead. I reached for her hands, and noticed that she was gripping something. I forced her hand open. A pill bottle fell to the floor.

"What is this, Shelly?" I asked as I bent over to pick it up. It was the prescription of pain medication the hospital had sent home with her earlier. I opened the bottle. There were only a few pills left. The label said there were originally fifteen tablets.

"How many of these did you take?" She didn't answer. Instead, she just slumped down to the floor beside the bathtub. "Shelly?" I snapped my fingers in her face. "How many? When did you take all of those pills?" I was beginning to cry. I was putting two and two together. I ran into her bedroom, grabbed some dry pajamas, and dialed Donovan as I did.

"Hey, babe. Is she okay?" he asked.

"No, Donovan. She's not. I think she tried to kill herself. She took twelve of the fifteen pain pills the hospital prescribed her," I cried. "What do I do? Call an ambulance?" I was beginning to panic.

"Is she responsive?"

"She isn't talking. She looks like a zombie. I found her in the bathtub with all of her clothes on and the water running all over the place. She wont talk. It's like she doesn't even know that I'm here," I explained.

"Call 911. Do it now, Angel. I'm on my way," he said, forcefully.

I called the police and an ambulance was dispatched. I changed Shelly's clothes, which was a struggle in itself. It was like trying to change an overgrown newborn baby. As I did so, I was crying, terrified for my best friend. Not only for her life, but for her mentality. I knew she was handling the loss of her baby too easily. She should have been set up with a grief counselor or something.

"Why would you do this, Shelly? Why would you try to take your life? I could have helped you," I whispered and attempted to brush her blonde locks. I knew she wasn't hearing anything I said. I keeping myself busy, trying to make her presentable. I didn't know why, but I didn't think she would appreciate strangers seeing her in a messy state. She always worried about the way she looks. I looked at her face, again. She was nodding off.

"Oh, no you don't! You stay awake, Shell! Don't you dare go to sleep on me." My voice broke as I started sobbing again. There was a pounding on the door and I stood to answer it. Donovan rushed into the apartment.

"Where is she?" he asked, pushing past me.

"In the bathroom. She can't walk, and I wasn't going to try to lift her. It was probably bad enough I changed her clothes," I explained. He stopped, turned toward me and put his hand on my cheek.

"Of course, you shouldn't try to pick her up, babe. You did good," he said as he kissed me quickly and went to the bathroom. Shortly after, he walked out with Shelly in his arms. "The paramedics are on the way, right?"

"Yes. They should be here any time now." As I said the words, there was a knock at the door. Donovan set Shelly down on the couch. I let the paramedics in.

"What did she take?" one of them asked. I handed him the bottle of the prescription pain medication and explained how many she had to have taken since I got her home from the hospital. "And why was she prescribed these?" he asked.

"She miscarried," I said, flatly. The paramedic nodded his understanding to me. As they were wheeling her out on the gurney, Cory was running up the walkway. Donovan must have called him.

"How is she?" he asked one of the paramedics. "Is she going to be okay?" He was searching Shelly for any signs of life.

"Her pulse rate is very low, and her breathing has almost stopped. We need to get her to the hospital as soon as possible, or we will lose her," the other paramedic was saying as they closed the door. They were gone within seconds.

Donovan, Cory, and I followed the ambulance to the hospital. As we sat in the waiting room, anxiously waiting for someone to tell us something, the little one inside of me bounced all over the place. I put my hand on my belly to calm him or her down.

"You should try to get some rest, Angel," Donovan said. He put his arm around my shoulder. I sighed.

"Not until I know what's happening to Shelly. Someone has got to know something by now." I couldn't stand it any longer. I stood and started toward the nurse's station. A doctor met me halfway.

"Excuse me. Are you here with Shelly McBride?" he asked. Finally, I thought.

"Yes," I said, breathlessly. "How is she?"

"Well, she is stable. We were able to reverse most of the effects of the medication. She's going to need a lot of rest, and in the near future, a lot of therapy. She is a very lucky lady. If you would have shown up twenty minutes later, she would not have made it to the hospital. She had to have taken all of those pills right before you arrived."

Wow, I thought. Shelly was going to be okay. Well, physically anyway. She would live. I could not make any sense of all the prior week's events leading up to this awful night. Shelly not only lost her baby, but felt she needed to take her own life as well. The Shelly I knew was always so happy and took everything lightly. She was never serious. This was all just so crazy to me. Thank God for Cory. If he hadn't called, I wouldn't have even known to go check on her.

"Thank you, doctor," I said. "Can we see her?"

"Yes, but only one person at a time, and only for a couple of minutes. Like I said, she needs to rest. She will most likely still be pretty out of it since a little bit of the medicine she took is still in her system," he replied.

I decided Cory should go in to see her first. That way she would know he cared deeply for her. Also, if she was mad at me for stopping her, then he would be able to let me know. Yes, I knew this was a little bit selfish of me. After ten minutes, Cory walked down the hall, toward where Donovan and I were sitting. Once again, the poor guy looked so exhausted he could fall over any minute.

"She wants to see you, Angel," he said, which came out more like a grumble. He ran his hand through his hair and sat down next to Donovan. I stood, and glanced at Donovan, who nodded his encouragement to me. I rewarded him with a small smile.

I finally reached Shelly's room which seemed to take forever. It was like a maze in this hospital, twists and turns everywhere. I knocked lightly on the closed door. I heard a small voice tell me to come in, so I slowly stepped inside. I closed the door behind me, and turned back to Shelly. I was almost afraid to look at her face, for fear of what I would see looking back at me. I decided I was okay with her being angry with me. I would rather have her mad at me than not be alive. I finally gathered the courage to look at her and was rewarded with a smile coming back to me. She sheepishly looked down at the sheets and shook her head, as if embarrassed.

"You really scared me, Shelly. Why would you do that? Did you seriously feel like that was your only option?" I mumbled as I made my way to the side of her bed. The tears came again at that moment. I was such a sap these days. It seemed like every time I turned around, the waterworks were on full blast. Shelly looked at me with tears of regret in her eyes.

"I'm so sorry, Angel. I don't know what I was thinking. It was as if I wasn't even in control of my body anymore." She sat up straighter in the bed. "I barely even remember taking the medicine. My last thought I was about my poor baby, that I, in a way, killed." I watched as the tears rolled down her cheeks. I shook my head in denial, and started to say something, but she put her hand up, stopping my words.

"I know what you're going to say, Ang," she continued, "but you're wrong. I put my baby, and myself, at risk because of that psychotic woman. I just knew she was going to hurt you. As I thought about that, I realized I would do it all over again. Then, I wondered if I should really be a mother, ever, because I couldn't even keep my baby safe when it was still inside of me." She fell silent so I decided it was okay for me to speak. I took a deep breath and began.

"Look, first of all, you did not kill your baby. It was a horrible thing none of us could see coming. Second, you will make an amazing mother someday, Shelly. You can't let something like this keep you from trying again." I hesitated for a second before continuing. "One last thing, though. Why didn't you talk to me about this? The last I checked, I was still your best friend. Why would you try to take your life instead of letting someone help you?" I demanded. Now that I knew she was going to be okay, I had to force myself from allowing anger to replace my fear.

Shelly took a deep breath. "I didn't think I was in that bad of shape, really. Sure, I was sad, but I figured it was a normal feeling. I remember telling Cory I needed some time alone, just to unwind. I don't know where that thought ended and suicidal thoughts began. Like I said, I don't really remember much. I'm so glad you found me," she cried. "I can't believe I took all of those pills. I would never do that. I must really need help, Angel."

"You can thank Cory for me finding you, Shell," I stated. "He's the one who called me and asked if I had talked to you. He didn't want to bug you, so I decided to go over there and check on you myself. As far as you getting help, I will get you set up with the therapist I see."

"Okay. That sounds good. Cory's such a good guy," Shelly mused aloud.

"He really is, Shelly. Not everyone would worry like he did. He seems to care about you a lot. I think he may be a keeper," I agreed.

"Yeah…" She sighed, and then yawned. I stood to leave, but she caught my hand. "Thank you, Angel. For coming over tonight. For being here, and for being my best friend. I'm so sorry you had to find me like that." She looked down at her shirt, then looked back up at me just as quickly. "Please tell me you are the one who changed my clothes?" I almost laughed at the mortified expression on her face at the thought of someone else seeing her naked. Yes, the Shelly I knew was back.

"I did." I said and she let out the breath she had been holding.

"Okay, good. Thank you again," she said during another yawn.

"No thanks needed, honey. I'm just glad that you are alright," I said as I was starting toward the door. I turned back to her. "Oh, and don't you ever do something like this to me again," I chastised.

"I'm going to be under surveillance for a few days. Something about a psychologist having to come in and assess me, or whatever." I walked out of her room. Shelly was going to get the help she needed. I wondered if this was some sort of post-partum depression or something like that. As I walked back to the waiting room, I was nervous at the thought of something similar coming over me after this baby was born. I have heard my fair share of horror stories about mothers like that.

# CHAPTER NINETEEN

It was one week before Christmas and I was finishing up my shift at the diner. Suzy, my boss, was basically pushing me out of the door, to Donovan's car. I was beginning to think she was more excited about this day than I was. Today was the day we were finding out the sex of the baby. Donovan and I hadn't even really talked about baby names. I guess I didn't exactly see the point of it until we knew what we were having.

Donovan was standing beside the passenger door, smiling, waiting for me to approach. I smiled back, kissed him, and got in the car. We were on our way to see the doctor. The baby must have sensed my excitement because he or she was going crazy inside of my belly. My insides were quickly becoming a punching bag.

"So, what are you hoping for? A boy or a girl?" Donovan asked, interrupting my thoughts. I figured he was checking to see if my mind had changed since the last time we had this talk.

"I don't honestly care, as long as he or she is healthy," I answered though still hoping secretly for a boy.

"Me too," he said as he let out his breath. He seemed nervous. I looked over at him, and noticed his knuckles were almost white from the grip he had on the steering wheel.

"Donovan, what's wrong with you?" I asked, his nervousness beginning to wear off on me. What could have him so worked up?

"Nothing. Nothing, really," he said as he glanced at me. Then he sighed. "Okay, maybe I'm nervous about finding out the sex. What if the doctors are wrong? What if we decorate the baby's room in pink, but when the baby comes out, he's a boy? Or the other way around?"

I laughed at the way he was rambling on. Knowing this was the only thing that worried him, I relaxed in my seat.

"Oh, babe," I said, "They have so much new technology these days, there is rarely a mistake like that anymore. They even have these 3-D ultrasounds so you see what the baby looks like."

"That's kind of creepy." he said. "I don't want to know what the baby looks like until it's born. Just that he or she is healthy is all."

I was still giggling when we checked into the doctor's office. We sat in the waiting room, and I glanced at the other women waiting as well. There was one girl, who seemed as if she were going to give birth any day now. She looked so sad, so alone, and afraid. She couldn't have been much older than eighteen, if even that. I decided right then, I wanted a boy for sure. I couldn't imagine having a daughter come home to me at such a young age, telling me she was pregnant. The thought made me shudder.

"Are you cold? Here, you can have my coat," Donovan offered. Instead of telling him the truth, I accepted his jacket. I didn't want to hear I was being silly for worrying about having a daughter. Sitting there, it hit me, the thought was a little ludicrous. I laughed inside.

"Miss Brady?" One of the nurses called my name. Donovan stood and offered his hand,to help me up as well. I smiled and took his hand. The nurse walked us to a room, asked me to change into a gown, and took my blood pressure. "Your blood pressure is a little high today, Angel," she mentioned. "Was the traffic bad?"

"No, the traffic was fine. I'm just a little nervous and excited is all," I laughed. She smiled and helped me lay back on the bed. She put the gel on my belly and started with the ultrasound.

"So, you want to know the sex?" she asked as she moved the wand around all over my stomach. Donovan and I smiled at each other.

"Yes," we said at the same time.

She went to work, taking measurements, and typing on the keyboard. I looked at the screen, and then looked at the nurse. Her brows were furrowed, as if confused.

"Is there something wrong?" I asked her. "Is everything okay with the baby?" I looked at Donovan, who shrugged his shoulders. He didn't see anything more than I did on that screen. The nurse made a few more movements with the wand, and then wiped my stomach off with a towel. She stood, and smiled at me.

"Everything is okay, Angel," she said. "I do, however, have to go get Doctor Ike. She will be able to talk to you about everything, okay?" Not leaving me with a chance to answer, she was out of the room. I looked back to Donovan who had the same look Fear. A knock on the door startled us. I tore my gaze from the ultrasound screen long enough to see who it was. It was Doctor Ike. She gave me a toothy grin.

"Hey there, Angel. Donovan," she said as she sat where the nurse was previously. "How are you feeling these days? Notice anything different?" She put more gel on my belly, and then the wand was back. She turned the volume up on the computer's speakers. Watery thumping sounds filled the room.

"I've been feeling great, actually. Just a little tired, but I'm assuming that is normal for pregnancy," I answered. "Doctor Ike? What's going on with the baby?" I couldn't wait any longer — I needed to know what was happening.

"Well, there's nothing going on with the baby," she began.

Donovan and I both breathed out a sigh of relief. "However, there is something going on with the *babies*." She waited long enough for what she had just said to sink in. It took at the very least, a full minute for her words to register in my brain. I looked at Donovan, again. He had gone pale. He quickly sat in the chair beside the bed. I worried about him, the doctor's words becoming very clear to me. I looked at Donovan, then the screen of the computer, then at the doctor, then back to Donovan. My eyes widened in the realization.

"Wait— What?! Did you say *babies*? As in more than one?" I asked. I looked back at Donovan. Doctor Ike laughed.

"Yes, there are two in there. Two heartbeats, two bodies, two heads, four legs, four arms, twenty fingers and toes." She turned the screen so that I could get a closer look.

Sure enough, I could see two babies on that screen. Twins. Donovan and I were having twins. I gazed at Donovan. He was staring at the screen, his pale face smiling.

"How did we not see this sooner?" I asked.

"Twins. Sometimes, it's hard to see them in an ultrasound. One can hide behind the other, and sometimes the heartbeats are the same, so it sounds like one," the doctor said and moved the wand again. "Offhand, it looks like twin boys. They are not shy at all." This made me laugh, even if it was a bit of a nervous laugh. Well, at least I wasn't having a girl, after all. "They are both extremely healthy, Angel." My heart finally slowed to a normal pace, as I wrapped my mind around everything she was saying. Two boys and they were healthy. Got it.

"Well, I guess that explains the weight gain. I thought I had a soccer player in there," I laughed, "but I wasn't exactly expecting two of them. No wonder it feels like I am constantly being beat up." Donovan finally broke out of his trance like state, and reached over, squeezing my hand.

"Now we have to figure out two names," he said and laughed.

"Yes, you do," the doctor continued. However, I was only half listening to her words. I was too busy thinking about baby boy names. "This does put you at a little bit of a higher risk, Angel. You are now five months along. Very rarely do twins go to full term. You need to watch for signs of early labor. Have you been having any cramping?" she asked.

"Sometimes, but not too much. It's usually only some back pain after working a long shift at the diner," I replied, thinking back at the horrible back pain I had after closing the restaurant last weekend. It was busy and I was miserable by the end of the night. When I got home, I took a hot shower and went to bed. The pain eased by morning, so I didn't think anything of it.

Doctor Ike sat silently, looking at the babies on the screen for a minute then turned to me, again. She looked at me with a very serious expression on her otherwise beautiful olive-colored face. By the look she was giving me, I felt I was about to be scolded for something—t like coming home past curfew when I was a kid to a very pissed off Grandma.

"Okay. Here's the deal. No more long shifts. If you feel like you must work at all, I want you to take multiple breaks. Listen to what your body is telling you, Angel. If it becomes painful, then you need to stop doing whatever it is causing the pain. That means, basically, if working is going to throw you into labor too soon, you will need to stop working. Do you understand what I am saying?" She turned to Donovan.

"Watch her. I can see she's very bull headed. You know her. You know her body language. If she is in pain, you need to make sure she isn't over-doing it. Got it?" she asked sternly. Both Donovan and I nodded our understanding, like two scolded children. "Okay then, do you two have any questions for me?" She looked from me to Donovan. She handed me a towel to wipe my stomach, again.

"No, I don't think so," I answered for both of us. Although, I was sure Donovan had a million questions running through his head. The goofy grin he had on his face was comical. I didn't want to laugh at him and embarrass him in front of the doctor, so I fought it off.

"Okay. I want to see you back in two weeks," the doctor said as she walked out of the room. I stood up, changed my clothes, and we walked to the car.

"Now where to?" Donovan asked.

"Well, I know we were thinking about having a reveal party to let everyone know the sex, but I was thinking we should go to Grandma's place," I said. He nodded and headed the car to my grandma's house. We rode in silence for a little while until I couldn't stand it any longer. "Are you going to say something?" He looked over at me and then pulled the car off of the road, putting it in park.

"I'm not sure what to say, really, Angel," he laughed. "I can't tell you how excited I am we are having two boys. I didn't want to tell you, because I was feeling guilty about thinking it, but I was terrified to have a little girl. I know dads are supposed to want girls, but I don't know the first thing about them." I reached over and put my palm on his cheek. I followed the action with a kiss .

"Want to know something?" I whispered. He nodded. "I didn't want a girl, either. When I saw that young girl in the waiting room, I couldn't imagine there being a chance of that girl being my daughter someday." I kissed him again as he laughed.

Donovan squeezed my hand. "Here I was, feeling all bad, and you were thinking the same thing as me." His gaze seemed distant.

"Sorry," I whispered. What could he be thinking? "What?" I asked out loud.

"I don't think you should work anymore," he blurted. I kind of knew, as soon as the doctor said the words, he would jump on me about work.

"I have to work, Donovan."

"No, you don't. I can easily support all of us."

"I'll get bored," I said, grasping at straws. I knew this was a losing battle. I would soon be telling Suzy I was going on early maternity leave.

"I'm not saying you can't do anything, babe. You can go and do as you please. I just don't want to worry about you going into labor early while refilling someone's coffee cup," he said.

"Fine," I conceded with a very loud sigh. He smiled, happy again. We were on the road again, heading to my grandma's. We turned on her street and I spotted her. She was just getting home herself. Donovan beeped his horn at her, and she turned, waving. Once parked, I stepped out of the car, into her comforting arms. Even as an adult, about to be a mother myself, everything became better in my grandma's arms.

"Well hello there, you two. It's cold out here and you're pregnant." She pulled the coat closer around me. "What brings you to my neck of the woods?" She had her arm entwined in mine as we walked up to her door. "And you be careful of the ice. I don't want you slipping."

"We have some news, Grandma," I answered. "About the pregnancy." Grandma looked worried until I smiled at her. Her features relaxed and she walked into the kitchen to start some hot chocolate. Since I was pregnant, she wouldn't make coffee anymore when we visited. She motioned for us to sit at the table while she took down three mugs from the cupboard. She soon joined us with all the mugs full of steaming hot cocoa.

"Alright, spill it. What's going on?" she asked as she sat. Donovan and I looked at each other. I nodded to him. I figured he would appreciate being able to tell someone the news, since he didn't have any family of his own. He cleared his throat.

"Do you know if twins run in your family? Or on Angel's

mom's side?" he asked, hinting. He was enjoying this. Grandma looked from him, to me, then back to him, shaking her head.

"No... I don't know of twins on either side," she stated. "Why?" Donovan didn't answer right away, so she looked back to me, confused. I looked back at her, intently, but didn't say a word. I just smiled.

It was like watching a cartoon in slow motion, watching my grandma, as realization took place in her mind. I could see confusion being replaced by understanding, which was soon replaced by shock.

"Oh my goodness!" She screamed. "You're having twins?" We both smiled and she jumped up from the table, almost knocking over her hot chocolate in the process. She jumped up and down and clapped her hands. It was so cute to see her so happy. "Boys? Girls? Both?" she asked.

"Boys," Donovan and I said simultaneously.

"Oh honey!" she exclaimed. "I'm so happy, but oh, so sorry at the same time. Boys are most definitely a handful." We all laughed at that. "We are going to be outnumbered now, Angel. Oh, now I can't wait to tell David. He is going to be so excited, too."

"Nah," Donovan argued. "We will be even."

"If you say so. Twin little boys should count as ten children," my grandma said as she typed into her phone. I don't think I'll ever get used to the fact she is up to date on technology. As if feeling my eyes on her, she looked up from her phone. "I have to tell David. You don't mind, do you?" I shook my head. I didn't mind at all.

I decided not to tell Shelly right away. I had talked to her every day since the suicide attempt, but I wasn't sure she was quite ready to hear this news. She was seeing a therapist and I didn't want to set her progress back in any way. She was doing so good. If she asked me, I wouldn't lie to her, of course, but I was definitely not going to offer any information. I would tell her when she was ready.

As the thoughts of Shelly filled my mind, it was as if she knew. She chose that moment to text me.

*"Hey, do you mind if Cory and I stop by later to visit you guys?" -S*
*"No. Not at all. It will be good to see you." -A*

I pushed 'send' and turned my attention back to the conversation between Grandma and Donovan. They were discussing boy names. Grandma liked William, Donovan Jr., Tyler, and Michael. Donovan laughed at the use of his name.

"I wouldn't do that to my poor kid," he said, standing. "If either of them are anything like I was, then he wouldn't be able to spell his name until he's in the third grade." We all laughed.

"I have my own secret to share with you both," Grandma said, her voice laden with amusement. I questioned her with my eyes. She knew what that look meant, so she continued. "David has asked me to marry him." She blurted the words out so fast, like if she didn't say them quickly, she would forget to tell me. Either that, or run out of nerve to tell me. I stood and hugged her tightly.

"That's great, Grandma!" I squealed. "Wait... I'm assuming you said 'yes.' Please tell me I'm right."

"Of course I said 'yes'." She proudly showed me her ring finger. On it was the most brilliant diamonds I had ever seen. As I was appraising the ring, I hadn't noticed the shared look that passed between my grandmother and my boyfriend.

"Oh, good. He's a good man, Mrs. Brady," Donovan had said.

"I'm sure he's a good man, Mrs. Brady," Donovan said.

"Yes, he sure is," she agreed and yawned. "Well, honey, I think

I need a nap. All of this exciting news... plus David wore me out last night." She winked at me. The thought made me shudder.

"Didn't need to know that, Grandma," I stated, " Anyway, we will let you get to that nap." I leaned in and kissed her on the cheek. "Love you. I'll call you tomorrow."

"Love you, too, sweetie," she said with a huge smile. "Congratulations!"

Donovan was still giggling about my grandma as we drove home.

"What's so funny?" I asked him, amused by his mood.

He shook his head.

"Nothing," he lied. I gave him a look that let him know I knew he wasn't being truthful. "Okay, okay. It's just that your grandma is so funny. I hope you and I are like that when we are her age."

"Who says you can put up with me for that long? Better yet, who says I can put up with you?" I asked, joking.

"I don't think I'll ever get enough of you," he said as he squeezed my hand. I smiled at him and looked out the car window. My thoughts soon traveled to Shelly and how I was going to tell her about the twins. I wasn't worried about her flipping out on me, but I was worried about her going into a depression. I couldn't help it. After her attempted suicide, I was always worrying about her.

"Same here, babe," I said.

When we pulled into the driveway, Cory's car was already there. I guess we had spent more time at Grandma's house than I thought. Shelly got out of the car and ran up to my door. I smiled as I wiggled my way out of the car.

"Hey, there! Whoa! Did you just pop out over night or something?" she asked as she took a good look at me. Shelly was in an exceptionally good mood.

"Or something," I mumbled as I hugged her and walked toward the front door.

"So?" She prodded as we all took our coats off and made ourselves comfortable in the living room. Donovan walked into the kitchen with Cory to make some hot chocolate.

"So, what?" I asked mischievously, knowing exactly what she wanted to know. She slapped me on the knee.

"Stop it! You know what!" she yelled. I laughed and turned toward her. Here goes nothing, I thought to myself, truly hoping she would take the news well. Shelly seemed to be doing much better these days. The doctors had put her on some anti-depression medicine, which looks like is really working.

"Well, I get to the doctor's office, and they set me up with the ultrasound. The nurse did her thing amd got really quiet. It scared the hell out of me. She left the room to get the doctor, but wouldn't tell Donovan or I anything. After a couple of minutes of waiting, the doctor finally came in," I said. Shelly looked at me with concern in her eyes. She was starting to show tears as well, so I figured I had better hurry up with my story.

"The doctor came in, and looked at the ultrasound, and well, we are having twins. Two boys." I waited for it to register in her head as I watched her face. Her features went from fear, to understanding, to excitement all within seconds.

"Twins?! Angel, oh my goodness! Twins? That is amazing news! Cory! They're having twins!" she yelled as she was bouncing with joy. I relaxed and allowed myself to be happy along with her. She took the news way better than I could ever hope for. Cory walked into the room with wonder on his face.

"Oh yeah? That's great news, guys. I'm so happy for you," he said, genuinely. Donovan walked in at that time with a tray full of mugs with hot chocolate. The babies must have sensed it and started doing summersaults. I smiled as I patted my stomach. An idea struck me right then. I stood and walked to the kitchen.

"Donovan," I called, "Could you help me with something really quick, please?"

"Sure," he replied and joined me in the kitchen. "What's up?"

"Since they are here, I was wondering what you would think about asking them to be the boys' godparents?" I figured Cory would be the best candidate since he and Shelly were doing so great. Plus, we really didn't have any other male friends. Donovan seemed thoughtful for a second.

"I think that sounds like a wonderful idea, babe," he said, kissed me on the cheek and turned back to the living room. "We should ask them now." I joined everyone else and took a sip of my hot, delicious drink. I cleared my throat and turned toward Shelly.

"Hey, Shell, I have something very important to ask you," I said. She looked at me with amusement in her eyes.

"Okay… What's up?" she asked. I looked at Donovan who nodded at me with encouragement.

"Well, Donovan and I were talking, and we were wondering if you would like to be the boys' godmother?" I asked, hesitantly. Shelly sat there, shocked, for what seemed like forever. We all waited, quietly. Finally, she looked me in the eyes, hers full of tears.

"I would be honored to be their godmother, Angel," she said as she squeezed me. "Thank you so much. You have no idea how happy this has made me." I smiled, and looked at Cory, who was sitting by a smiling Donovan.

"Cory, we also would love for you to be their godfather," I said. He looked up at me quickly. I had shocked them both tonight, I thought, almost laughing.

"Really?" he asked, blushing. "I would like that, as long as Shelly is okay with it." He looked over at her. She had a confused look on her face.

"Why would I need to approve, Cory?" she asked as she stood, walked over to him, and sat on his lap. He wrapped his arms around her waist. "Of course I would be okay with that. Who better?" She giggled. He stood, holding her in his arms, and sat her on his chair. He knelt down in front of her.

"Well, I would need your approval because… I have something else to ask you…" He reached into his pocket. "I figured since tonight we are in a celebrating mood, I could add another thing to celebrate about. Shelly, would you do the honor of becoming my wife?"

I almost fell over in my seat, and it looked as if both Donovan and Shelly were close to doing the same. Shelly sat, a smile frozen on her face, but said nothing. I cleared my throat, loudly, to break the trance she was in.

"Oh, um, wow, Cory…" She looked at me and I smiled, nodding. "Of course I will marry you, baby." Her laugh turned into a squeal as she was picked up and swung around by Cory. He set her back down and slid the ring on her finger.

"This has turned out to be such an amazing night," I said to Donovan as joined me on the couch. He reached over and grabbed my hand in his.

"It really has. The only thing to make it better is if you call work tomorrow and tell them you are going on early maternity leave," he said. I gave him the 'don't tell me what to do' look, which made him laugh. "Okay. Okay, I won't push it just yet, but you heard what the doctor said. We want these boys, and their momma, to be healthy. Don't want them coming too soon, babe."

"I know. I want to at least give them a two week notice. I mean, I'm still feeling okay. I just can't work any more long shifts."

"I can live with that," Donovan said, kissing my neck.

I made it just over two weeks. Suzy was kicking me out early every day, saying we were slow and I wasn't needed. I swore she and Donovan were in on this whole thing together. To be honest, was alright with being done working. My feet were starting to swell, and I was becoming tired a lot easier than normal. On my last shift, all of the girls at the diner threw me a little baby shower after we closed. They gave be all kinds of goodies for the babies. Suzy bought the boys two car seats which was great. At least we had something to bring them home in. As we were cleaning everything up, Suzy approached me with an envelope in her hands. She handed it to me, but said not to open it until after I had gotten home.

Finally comfortable on the couch, I opened the envelope. It was two policies from the bank. The note inside said they were accounts set up for the twins' college funds. As I cried, I called Suzy and thanked her. She was such a sweet woman.

# CHAPTER TWENTY

I was washing the dishes and I swear these two boys inside of me were already fighting. I was thirty-two weeks into the pregnancy. I was huge, always bumping into things, and just plain uncomfortable. While putting the glasses into the cupboard, I felt a huge jab of pain in my lower back.

"Okay, boys, you really need to settle down in there. You're hurting your momma," I said, rubbing my belly. I put my hand on my back and waddled to the kitchen table. I looked out the window, finally seeing signs of life outside. The trees were budding, and the grass was peeking out of the melting snow. It was a very welcome sight after a horrible winter. March was one of my favorite months. It always seemed to be the month that ended winter. Sure, every now and then, it would still snow a little in March. For the most part, though, it was the beginning of warm weather. As I thought about the weather, another pain hit me, this time in my lower abdomen, and it took my breath away.

I stood from the table and walked into the living room. I laid down on the couch, putting my feet up, and turned on the television. The doctor had said I would have pre-labor pains closer to the end of my pregnancy. She had said they would usually come when I was overdoing it. Yesterday, I washed all of the baby clothes, put them away, and put all of the bedding on the cribs. Today, I scrubbed down the kitchen and bathroom. I guess you could say I did a little bit too much and my body was not happy about it.

I dozed off for a little while, but then was awakened by another stabbing pain. I sat up quickly. As I did, there was a gush of something coming from down below. I looked down, and the couch was soaked. I gathered my water broke.

Trying not to panic, I reached for my cell phone. I dialed Donovan's phone number, but got his voicemail. He must have been busy. I decided to call the police department. I could at least leave him a message there, and know he would get it right away. It only rang one time.

"Officer Bradner, can I help you?"

"Hey, Rick, it's Angel. Is there any way you can get a message to Donovan for me, please?" I asked.

"Yeah, sure. How are you, by the way? Should be about ready to have those babies pretty soon, right?" Rick asked.

"I'm doing okay. Thank you. Actually, the reason I'm calling is because I'm at home and my water just broke. I need to either have Donovan come and get me, or meet me at the hospital," I explained.

"Oh shit! Okay! I'll get a hold of him right away, honey. Do you need a ride to the hospital. Should I send an ambulance?" He went into professional mode.

"Thanks, Rick, but no. I'm pretty sure I have enough time to find someone. Just please get that message to Donovan as soon as you can," I said then hung up just as another pain hit me, doubling me over. I realized quickly these were not pre-labor pains. These were contractions, and they were only about five minutes apart. After the pain subsided, I called Shelly. She answered right away.

"Hey, Ang. What's up?" I could hear other voices in the background. My heart fell. She was doing something, and she was my only hope, other than calling for an ambulance, and I didn't want to do that.

"Shelly, please tell me you're not busy. I have a problem. My water just broke and I'm having some massive contractions. Donovan's at work and I can't get a hold of him. How fast can you be here?" I rushed.

"Oh no. Um… I'm at the mall, but I can be there in about ten minutes. Can you wait that long?" She asked. I could tell in her voice she was freaking out.

"Yeah, my contractions are about five minutes apart. I'm sure these little guys can wait until you.…. OH!" I yelled as another contraction hit . I wished now I had let Donovan talk me into taking the birthing classes. At the time, though, I didn't think I needed them. Women had been having babies for centuries without being told how to breathe. I breathed through it, and continued, weakly, "Just hurry, please, Shell."

"I'm in my car already, honey." I ended the call, and then called Grandma. She didn't answer so I left her a message to meet me at the hospital. As I was putting my jacket on, another contraction had hit me. This one stopped me dead in my tracks. I reached over, and held on to the back of the recliner and squeezed it. The contractions were getting closer together, and harder. After the last one ended, I went to the laundry room and picked up some new clothes, so I could change. I grabbed the bag I had packed for the hospital and waited for Shelly to get here. My phone rang. It was Donovan.

"Hello," I said, breathlessly.

"Hey, babe. Sorry I missed your call. I was out on a run. I got the message from Rick. He radioed me. I'm on my way. I can be there in about twenty minutes," he said quickly.

"It's okay. Actually, Shelly will be here any minute. Just meet us at the hospital, okay? My contractions are getting closer to every three minutes now. I don't think I can wait twenty minutes, babe." Shelly barged through the door. She took my bag from me, and helped me off of the couch.

"Okay. I'll be there as soon as I can," I barely heard him say as another pain sliced through my stomach. "And Angel? I love you."

I dropped my phone during the contraction. The pain becoming so intense I could no longer focus on anything. When I got in the car, I looked down. There was blood on Shelly's seat. I started to cry.

"Shelly, I'm ruining your seats," I said.

"Don't you worry about my seats," she said as she looked down to where I was staring. "Oh, God, Angel. You're bleeding!"

"I know. I'm so scared. It's still too soon for them to come. What if something's wrong? I don't think there's supposed to be blood." I could hear the panic in my voice.

"Don't you worry about that. Those babies are going to be just fine, sweetie. There's all kinds of not-so-pretty things involved with having babies." That was the last thing I heard. I passed out.

"Angel? Angel, honey, you have to wake up. These babies can't come out without your help," I heard, faintly. I opened my eyes. I saw my doctor in between my legs. She had a hold of one knee, and Shelly had the other. "I need you to push, Angel. Push!" she yelled. I pushed. "Great, you're doing great." I could feel a huge pressure, and I pushed harder.

That's when I heard my first baby's cry. As soon as I heard that, someone else rushed into the room. I felt myself relax as I realized it was Donovan. Just then, another contraction came. The first baby was handed off to a nurse. I tried to watch what she was doing with him, but the urge to push overcame any other thoughts. Another pressure followed, and then another cry. Donovan arrived just in time to cut this one's cord.

"Great job, Angel," the doctor said. "Now I need you to stop pushing. You have two good looking little boys over there." She smiled and nodded toward the other side of the room. I followed her gaze to where the nurses rushed to clean the babies up.

I looked up and smiled at Donovan, who was saying something to the doctor. I couldn't make out what was being said. The doctor said something back, and then Donovan walked over to the babies.

As I was trying to see what was going on with the twins, my vision became blurry. I was also freezing, all of a sudden. I looked over at Shelly, and she looked back at me, terrified. What was going on? Why was everyone freaking out? Were the babies alright? I struggled to keep my eyes open.

"She's losing way too much blood," the doctor said anxiously. "I have to get this stopped or we are going to lose her. I'm going to have to prepare her for emergency surgery."

"Angel, don't you dare leave me," Donovan said, running back to my side. "You have to stay with me, babe. I can't do this alone..." His voice faded. I couldn't hear him. Nor anyone else.

"I'm c-cold," I tried to say. I don't know if the words ever made it out of my mouth, or not. My teeth were chattering. The last thing I rememberedwas my teeth were going to shatter and my boys would have a mom with dentures. Silly, I knew.

I woke up to a familiar, annoying, beeping noise. I looked around the room and spotted my little boys. They looked so tiny in their little bassinets. I went to reach for them, but the pain in my stomach stopped me.

"Hey, you," a soft voice said. I saw Donovan walking toward me. "It's about time you woke up and met your little men. We have missed you." He leaned down and kissed my forehead.

"Baby one was four pounds, and baby two was four pounds, three ounces.

"How long have I been out? What happened? I barely remember giving birth," I croaked. Donovan handed me some water, which I drank greedily. "Thank you."

"About three days now," he answered. "We almost lost you, babe. Again," he choked out. "You have got to stop doing this. My heart can't take it."

"How? I mean, what exactly happened?" I asked, trying to piece together all of the events that had taken place. Three days? I had already missed out on three days of my boys' lives? "Can you bring them to me, please?" Donovan nodded and rolled the bassinets up to the side of my bed.

"You almost bled to death, Angel. You had to have surgery to save your life?" he started to explain.

"What kind of surgery?" I asked, focusing on the two little pieces of perfection beside me. I counted all fingers and toes. They were all there. Exactly alike, except one had a small birthmark in between his eyebrows. I looked up at Donovan.

"Look what we did," I said to him. He smiled down at me.

"You did most of the work there, babe," he said, shaking his head. "As far as the surgery…" As his words trailed off, I looked up, quickly. Donovan continued. "She had to take everything, Angel, to stop the bleeding."

"What do you mean 'everything'?" I asked. What could she have taken that would be killing me? Suddenly, I realized what he was trying to say to me. I immediately started to cry. She had to give me a hysterectomy. I was not going to be having any more children. I automatically felt empty inside. It was as if my womanhood had been taken away.

"Hey, hey. Don't cry, babe. It's going to be okay. At least we have our boys. Who, by the way, still don't have names," Donovan consoled. He was right. I had twins. It wasn't like I was really planning on having any more children. It was just the thought of the choice being taken away from me that bothered me.

"You're right. We need to pick names out for these guys," I said, thankful for the distraction. I wiped my face with the backs of my hands.

"Well, I had a lot of time to think while you were out. I was thinking, I kind of really like the name Braxton. Braxton Mancini. It has a nice ring to it, doesn't it?" he asked.

"I like it. Okay, so Braxton it is. As for the other, how about Brody?" I asked. Donovan's face lit right up.

"I love it. Braxton and Brody Mancini. Perfect names for perfect little boys," he said, excitement shining in his eyes.

"Wow, look who's finally decided to wake up from her beauty sleep," Shelly said as she walked into the room. She immediately walked over to Braxton's bassinet and picked him up before sitting down. "How are you feeling, Ang? You really scared us this time. Don't ever do that again, young lady," she scolded. I smiled. Shelly was completely back to herself again.

"I'm okay. I didn't exactly plan on this, you know," I laughed. "But, don't you worry. I won't do that again."

"I know," she replied. "It was just really scary seeing you like that, that's all. It's hard seeing the strongest person you have ever known suffer like that."

"So have you decided on any names yet?" A voice interrupted. Grandma decided to make her grand entrance at that moment. She picked Brody up, and sat down beside Shelly. I could see I was going to have constant competition for my children. The thought made me smile. In my eyes, you couldn't ever have too many people loving your child.

"Actually, yes, right before you two got here," Donovan said. "Shelly, you are holding Braxton, and Grandma, you are holding

Brody." His voice was so full of love and pride, my heart almost exploded.

"I love the names!" Shelly squealed, scaring Braxton awake. He started to whimper, so she brought him to me. I decided to try to feed him. He calmed down as soon as he was in my arms, eating hungrily.

I yawned, and Grandma stood, bringing Brody to me. I handed Braxton to Donovan, who put him back in his bassinet. He was out like a light. Brody had a harder time feeding. It took a few tries before he understood what he was supposed to do. Eventually, though, he got it and fell fast asleep during his meal. Donovan took him and laid him down in his bassinet. I was almost asleep, myself.

"Well, honey, I think I'm going to get out of here and let you get some more rest. You're sure going to need it before you get out of here," my grandma said as she put her jacket on. "I'll come by tomorrow to see you." She leaned down and placed a kiss on the top of my head. "Love you, my Angel."

"Okay. Love you, too, Grandma," I said, in mid-yawn. Shelly stood up, as well.

"Yeah, I'm going to get out of here, too. I have wedding invitations to get mailed out," she said as she winked at me. She leaned down and placed tiny kisses on each of the babies' heads. I smiled at her sweet gesture.

When it was just Donovan, the boys, and I left in the room alone, I decided I wanted to try to take a shower. Donovan pushed the call button on the bed.

"I'm definitely not letting you do that alone this time, babe," he said sternly. I couldn't blame him. This wasn't like the last time, and I honestly didn't think I wanted to try it alone, anyway.

The nurse came in and confirmed that I was, by no means, to get out of the bed by myself just yet. She helped me to the bathroom, and sat me on the shower chair. It was an amazing shower and I actually felt like a million dollars when I finally finished. I stepped out of the bathroom to find Donovan walking around with one of the boys in his arms, talking to him.

"Okay, Braxton, I'm going to need your help with this one, buddy. If this is going to work, Mommy needs to know how much we love her."

"If what is going to work?" I asked as I approached them, slowly. I was still very tender. When I heard I had surgery, I was terrified I would have a huge scar on my stomach. I was relieved when I looked down, in the shower, and there was only a tiny incision. Doctor Ike was amazing. I startled Donovan when I spoke. He jumped and turned around quickly, blushing.

"Oh... Nothing... Braxton and I were just having ourselves a little talk is all," he explained. There was a knock on the door. Doctor Ike walked in.

"Hey, Angel. How are you feeling?" she asked as she neared the bed.

"Hello, Doctor Ike. I'm feeling much better now that I've taken a shower," I said. She pulled up my gown to check my incision.

"The incision looks great. I just checked your latest blood work. It looks good now, too," she said as she sat down at the computer in my room. "I'm thinking, if you're feeling up to it, you could probably go home tomorrow." She turned back to me. I could have hugged her at that moment. I wanted nothing more than to take my babies home and get everyone settled in.

"I would like that, Doctor," I said, excitedly.

"I'm sorry I had to do a hysterectomy, Angel," she started, "but if I hadn't you would have not been able to meet those little cuties over there." She pointed at the twins.

"I understand," I said, and I did understand. It was a matter of life and death. I was glad she chose to save me, so my boys wouldn't be forced to grow up without their mother, like I was. She stood and walked to the door.

"Okay. Well, then, I guess I will see you in six weeks for a check-up?" she asked.

"Sounds good." I said as she let herself out. I turned my attention back to Donovan. "I think I need a nap." He laughed and agreed. He walked over, tucked the blankets around me and sat beside the bed.

"We will all still be here when you wake up, babe."

"You had better, be," I said as I dozed off.

# CHAPTER TWENTY-ONE

I was giving Brody a bath when my cell phone rang. I decided to let the voicemail pick it up and turned my attention back to the task. He was smiling and cooing at me as I dribbled water over his belly. I looked over at Braxton, who was sitting in his bouncy seat, patiently waiting his turn. Both of the twins loved their baths. They were just like their momma in that area. In every other area, though, they were their daddy. They both had his dark hair, and bright blue eyes. I was glad for that.

As I pulled Brody out of the tub and was drying him off, Braxton ran out of patience. He started to whimper. I quickly put lotion, powder, and a diaper on Brody and sat him down in his seat, then scooped Braxton up.

"Okay, little man. It's your turn now," I was saying as I undressed him.

"When is it going to be my turn, Mom?" Donovan joked from the doorway. He reached down and picked Brody up. "You're going to be one handsome little devil in that tiny tuxedo your Aunt Shelly got you for her wedding."

"Yes, he sure is. They both are," I said while washing up Braxton. Shelly's wedding was in a few hours. She and Cory had decided on an outside wedding, and they couldn't have picked a better day to have it. It was a sunny summer day.

"I can't wait to see their momma in her dress," Donovan said. I blushed. It hadn't taken me very long to lose the weight from the babies, but I was still self-conscious about wearing the dress Shelly had picked out for me. It was quite revealing. I think she did it on purpose, because she knew she wouldn't be able to get me into something like that for any other reason. The color was beautiful, though. It was a royal blue.

I finished up with Braxton's bath, and picked him up. As I laid him down on the towel I had set out, Donovan took over the task of finishing him up. I was so thankful he was a hands-on dad. He didn't let me do anything alone if he was around. I honestly didn't think I could do it alone.

When we arrived at the park for the wedding, I left the boys with Donovan, Grandma and David, and went into the building to help Shelly get ready. Plus, I'd put on my dress, as well. When I found her, she was sitting in front of a mirror, staring at her reflection. Her face lit up as soon as she saw me walk in.

"Hey! Thank God, you're here. I have a serious problem on my hands," she called out as I neared. "This wedding just isn't going to work." I stopped dead in my tracks.

"What do you mean, 'This wedding isn't going to work'?" I asked, starting to worry. She couldn't be getting cold feet. Of course, this was Shelly I was talking to. She never ceases to surprise me, even after all of these years.

"I have something old, something new, and something blue… But I don't have anything borrowed, Angel. I can't go through with this wedding without something borrowed. The marriage won't last," she whined. I almost laughed until I noticed how genuinely worried she was. Leave it to Shelly to be so superstitious.

"Hmmm… Let me think. What can you borrow?" I said as I

tried to think of something. An idea came to me. "I have just the thing. Let's get your dress on, and I'll give it to you." She looked at me, suspiciously, but agreed to put her dress on.

Shelly made a gorgeous bride. She had picked out a strapless, white, wedding dress. It had sequins on the breast and then a lacey design going all the way down the train. I stared in awe when she faced me.

"You look beautiful, sweetie," I whispered. She beamed at me in the mirror. I reached around my neck, and pulled off the necklace I was wearing. It was Grandma's, until she gave it to me a few years ago. It was made of white gold, and had a single diamond pendant. I put it on Shelly who smiled gratefully.

"It's perfect. Thank you, Angel," she said, tearing up.

"Don't cry, Shell. You'll ruin your make up and we don't have time to do it again," I said, trying not to cry, myself. I heard the music begin. "It's time, honey." Shelly took a deep breath, and nodded. I grabbed my bouquet and headed out of the building, toward the small group of people seated. I yanked on the hem of my much-too-short dress, and walked down the aisle. I caught a glimpse of Donovan who was sitting with his mouth wide open. My grandma had noticed, and elbowed him. He straightened up, smiling sheepishly. I just shook my head and giggled.

Shelly and Cory had a very nice, yet simple, ceremony and reception. Donovan and I had left early as the twins were getting tired. I, personally, just wanted to get out of the dress and heels I was wearing.

After we put the boys to bed, Donovan and I dropped onto the couch at the same time. We looked at each other and burst out laughing.

"What a day," I said as I lay my head on his shoulder.

"For sure," he said, rubbing my thigh. I looked up into his eyes and smiled.

"How about a bath?" I asked.

"Sounds good to me," he answered and was picking me up before I could say anything else. I picked up the baby monitor off of the table as we passed it.

Our bath was glorious. We took turns washing each other and massaging. We made love that night, uninterrupted, for the first time since the boys were born. Donovan took his time with me, making sure I was fully satisfied. As I lay in his arms that night, I knew I was going to love this man until the day I died. Which, hopefully, wasn't going to be until we were both old and gray.

A week later, I was making breakfast, when the phone rang. I walked into the living room, and picked it up.

"Hello?"

"Hey, Angel, it's me," Shelly whispered on the other end.

"What's up? Why are you whispering? And shouldn't you be enjoying your honeymoon?" I asked.

"Well, we are enjoying our honeymoon. It's just that, I needed to talk to you," she said quietly.

"Okay, well, you have me. What's going on, Shell?" I asked again.

"I had to tell you, well, I'm late again. I knew before the wedding, but I haven't even told Cory yet. That's why I'm whispering. I have the test. I brought it with me," she said.

"So what are you waiting for? Take it!" I laughed.

"I was waiting for you. I didn't want to take it alone. I needed you here with me. At least, in spirit, or on the phone," she mused. That made me laugh again.

"Okay, so you have me there with you. Pee on the stick. It's not like it's the first time you've peed while on the phone with me," I said, giggling.

"I'm scared. What if it's negative? I want a baby so bad," she was saying, but I could hear the wrapper of the test being opened.

"It'll be okay, Shell. If it's negative, then you try again. It doesn't mean anything," I consoled.

"Okay, it's done. Now we wait." I heard the toilet flush. She went silent, though I could hear her breathing. I waited, silently, with her. Then I heard a gasp.

"What is it? What does it say?" I asked.

"It's positive. I'm pregnant, Angel!" she yelled. The relief I felt at that moment almost took me to my knees. I started crying silently, happily.

"That's amazing, Shelly. I'm so, so happy for you. Now, you need to go tell Cory," I said as I went back to finishing making breakfast. I started to heat up the twins' bottles when she squealed in my ear.

"Cory!" she yelled. "Guess what? I'm pregnant!" I could hear his muffled voice in the background. "Yes!" she yelled again, laughing. I heard him hoot loudly, and laughed.

"I'm going to let you go now, Shelly. You two celebrate, and we will talk again when you get home. Love you," I said.

"Thank you so much, Angel. You're the best friend I could ever have asked for. Thank you for being here for me. I love you!" She hung up.

I was still laughing when Donovan appeared in the kitchen with a baby in each arm.

"What's so funny?" he asked as he sat. I grabbed Brody from him and started to feed him, handing the other bottle to Donovan.

"Oh, I just got off of the phone with Shelly," I started to say. I took a bite of my eggs, and then continued. "She called me so I could be there with her while she took a pregnancy test." I giggled. Donovan smiled, and perked up.

"And?"

"And it was positive. She's pregnant."

"That's awesome!" he shouted. Braxton stopped sucking on his bottle and looked at his dad, brows furrowed. Donovan smiled down at him.

"Sorry, buddy," he said more quietly. Braxton continued with his meal.

"Yeah, she is so happy. So is Cory," I said.

"I bet they are both ecstatic," he replied.

"They are. Anyway, so what is on our agenda for today?" I asked as I burped Brody. Donovan was doing the same with Braxton.

"Well, I was thinking, since it's so nice out, maybe we could go to the park. We could take the stroller and all of us can get some fresh air," he said, standing.

"I think that is a great idea," I said, doing the same.

An hour later, we were packed up, and on our way to the park. We had packed lunches and everything else we would need for a day with nature. As we were walking, Donovan had stopped, knelt down, and tied his shoe. When I looked back at him, he was watching me, intently.

"What?" I asked, amused. He motioned for me to walk back to him. I turned the stroller around and started back. "Are you okay?"

"Yeah, there's just something over here I want to show you. It's pretty cool," he said as he looked over to his right. As I neared him, I looked in the same direction that he was. I didn't see anything. I looked back at him, confused.

"What are you talking about? I don't see any—" My words were cut short when I looked at him again. He reached in his pocket and pulled out a little pouch. He held on to my hands.

"Angel, I know we have been through some rough patches, and life has been crazy for the past year, but you mean the world to me. I love you with my whole heart. I can't, won't, picture my life without you in it. I want to keep you safe and I want to spend the rest of my life showing you how happy you make me. Will you marry me?" he finished, pulling a diamond ring out of the pouch, holding it up for me to see.

I stood there, looking down at him in shock. I knew I needed to say something, but the words wouldn't come out of my mouth. I loved this man —that much I knew. Could I see myself spending the rest of my life with him? Yes, of course I could. I couldn't imagine my life without him. I looked down at what he was offering me. The ring was absolutely beautiful and looked vaguely familiar. I looked back into his eyes as he knelt there in front of me, waiting, full of hope.

"Yes. Yes of course I'll marry you, Donovan!"

He slid the ring on the ring finger of my left hand and picked me up. He swung me around and I laughed. The twins, who were sleeping a few minutes ago, chose that moment to remind us of their presence. I turned back to them and quieted them down. They were silent as soon as they noticed their dad and I hadn't abandoned them.

"You have just made me the happiest man in the world. I hope you know that." He was grinning from ear to ear now. His boyish reaction made him that much more handsome.

"I looked down at the ring on my finger. The diamond was huge. "This must've cost a fortune, Donovan. You didn't have to get one so big."

"You'd be surprised at how cheap I got this, babe," he said secretively. I looked at him, questioning him with my eyes. He laughed. "Doesn't that stone look familiar to you?"

"I thought it did, but I wouldn't know why," I said quietly while thinking. We started to walk again, heading toward the picnic tables to each lunch and change the boys.

"Well, remember that diamond earring we found on the beach in Florida?" He barely got the words out before the light bulb went on in my head. That's where I'd seen it before!

"Of course, but when we went to the police station, they said they were going to hold onto it until someone claimed it."

"Remember?" he asked as he stepped closer. "They said they would only hold it for a month, and then, if someone didn't claim it, it would be ours. A while back, the police station called me and told me they didn't think anyone was coming for it since it had been over a few months. They asked me if we were still interested. I said yes, so they shipped it overnight to my place. I took it to a jeweler when I was released from the hospital after being shot, asked if he could set the diamond in a ring, and you know the rest." He was so proud of himself, I nearly laughed. Instead, I kissed him. That's why he was being so sneaky when they released him. I thought it was odd he had gotten a ride from someone else. He had really planned this out.

"You are so amazing," I said, as I hugged him tightly. I leaned my cheek on his chest, listening to his steady heartbeat. I couldn't believe everything he had done to make sure this day would be perfect. The fact the twins were here to see it, made it even better.

"You are the one who is amazing. I knew, while we were in Florida, we were meant to be together. We just fit." He lifted my chin so he could kiss me, deeply.

"Yes, we sure do. Like peanut butter and jelly, or macaroni and cheese," I said, not being able to stop the laughter at my own humor. Donovan joined in on my laughter.

"Yep. Like both of those. I love you so much, Angel."

"I love you, too. Grandma is going to love this phone call. So, when do you want to do this?" I said as we walked back to the car, to head home.

"I'd like to as soon as possible. I think I have had to wait long enough for you to be my wife. I don't want to wait anymore," he said.

"Well, how about July? I'd like to do something outside, like Shelly and Cory did."

"Sounds good to me," he said as he buckled Braxton into his car seat. I smiled, planning the whole thing in my head.

I decided I couldn't wait to call Grandma, and tell her my good news. I knew she would be thrilled. So, on the way home, I looked in the back seat to see if the boys were still sleeping. When I was sure they were, I pulled my cell phone out of my purse, and dialed her number. I put it on speaker so Donovan could hear her reaction to our news.

"Hey, honey! How are you? And my great-grandbabies?" she asked right away.

"We are all doing great, Grandma. How are you?" I answered.

"We are, too. David and I were just trying to figure out when to plan our wedding. When do you think would be a good time to get married?" she asked. I grinned.

"Well, actually, Donovan and I were just talking about that and we think July would be the perfect time to get married," I hinted.

"July, you say? It's so hot in July, though. You and Donovan were talking about when David and I should tie the knot?" She was putting two and two together.

"No, we were talking about when we should get married," I said, trying to help her along. She was quiet, so I decided to just go ahead and tell her. "Donovan asked me to marry him today, Grandma."

"Oh! That is great! Congratulations you two!" she hollered in my ear. "David! Donovan and Angel are getting married, too! Wait... I have an idea. Why don't we all get married together? Or would that take your special day away from you? Because I don't want to do that..." I laughed, as did Donovan. I looked over at him, and he smiled and nodded.

"Oh, it wouldn't take anything from us, Grandma. Donovan and I think that sounds like a great idea. But, you would have to be willing to get married in July. We don't want to wait any longer than that," I explained.

"Okay, honey. July it is." She giggled. "Who would have thought I would be getting married at the same time as my granddaughter?" Her giggles turned into fits of laughter, which of course, made Donovan and I laugh as well. Finally, we all composed ourselves long enough to finish our conversation. We decided we would talk the next day and start to plan our double wedding day.

# CHAPTER TWENTY-TWO

I didn't tell Shelly about the engagement until she and Cory got home from their honeymoon. I refused to take any of the attention from her happiness. When I did finally tell her, she gave me a hard time about keeping it from her, at first. She was ecstatic, of course. She was worried, however, she wouldn't be able to fit into the dress I had picked out for her. Leave it to Shelly to be worried about what she would look like, I thought. After that crazy short thing she made me wear to hers — she had nothing to worry about, though. I chose a peach sundress for her that flowed out at the waist. I wasn't going to put her through the same thing, making her feel self- conscious.

We all chose to get married in Florida since that was where Donovan and I started our relationship. Grandma and David were more than happy to join us, being as neither one of them had been to St. Augustine. Hearing everything I had told her about it, Grandma was excited to see for herself what all of the fuss was about.

We had a beach wedding in July. It was a simple, yet very nice, ceremony, just a block away from The Fountain of Youth. Donovan threatened to call off the wedding if he saw even one peacock. We didn't, but I would have loved to have seen his face if one did pop up. I almost thought about planning for it to happen, actually. I thought better of it.

Grandma made a beautiful bride. She and I wore matching white sundresses, and we were both barefoot. Her short, white, hair was decorated in a diamond crown, whereas I wore my hair down. The best part was, however, the radiant beam of happiness her face as we walked down the aisle toward our future husbands. She began to glow when she had made eye contact with David. I could not remember ever seeing my grandma so happy, and it made my heart swell even bigger than it was.

Cory, the poor guy, was stuck with one of the twins, while Shelly held the other during the vows. They were both at the squirmy ages, neither of them wanting to sit still for more than two minutes. Shelly told Cory it would be great practice for their own baby someday soon. I watched him, as he was sweating, trying to keep a hold of Brody, as he wanted to be everywhere other than where he was. I laughed as I noticed his struggle. I took Brody from him, as soon as I said 'I do.'

After the ceremony, we had dinner at a popular beach restaurant. It was really nice, and not as busy as I had thought it would be. This was prime beach-going season, and it was a Saturday. As I looked around, I thought about how slow they were. They should have been slammed. I mentioned something to Donovan who smiled guiltily.

"I may, or may not, have reserved half of the restaurant for our little dinner party," he confessed.

"Well, I'm glad you did. Thank you. This is nice," I said, kissing him. He grinned and went to work on the dish in front of him. Shelly chose that moment to stand up, and clanked her sparkling cider-filled glass with a spoon. The entire restaurant grew quiet, both sides.

"I would like to propose a toast," she said, smiling from ear to ear. Once she had everyone's attention, she continued. "I just want to say that, in all of the years I have been best friends with Angel, I never, in a lifetime, thought we would all be where we are today. Angel, I am so happy for you, honey. You deserve the best, and it looks like you've got the one that is the best for you. It is so nice to see you happy, as you have brought so much joy to other peoples' lives." She smiled at me, tears filling her eyes. My eyes filled as well.

"Thank you, Shelly," I said.

"You're welcome, but I'm not done yet. Donovan, you are the luckiest man alive. I know you will treat my best friend like gold. You have already proven your worth." Shelly focused her attention on Grandma and David. "Grandma, I am so happy you were able to find love again, after all of these years. You deserve happiness more than anyone else in this room. Angel wouldn't be who she is today if it weren't for you, and we all owe you a deep debt for that. Thank you, and congratulations to all of you!" She ended the toast with a bang.

"Here, here!" We all cheered and drank our champagne to Shelly's toast. The twins yawned. Shelly and Cory offered to take them to her parent's place with them in Miami. It took some coercing from both Shelly and Donovan for me to agree, but I finally did. We were putting together all of their things when Shelly and Cory came to the hotel door.

I handed the car seats to Cory, and Donovan followed him out to the car so he could show him how to strap them in. While they were out there, Shelly pulled me out onto the back balcony.

"Before we leave, I had to tell you. The ultrasound showed I was further along than we had originally thought. Looks like we will be having a New Year's baby. Anyway, we found out we are having a girl. Cory and I have already chosen a name for her.

Her name will be Angela Marie, after both you and my mom," she stated, proudly. My eyes filled with tears, for the third time that day.

"That is so cool, Shelly. Thank you," I said as I squeezed her. To me, there was no better honor than to have a child named after you. This was a gift from Shelly I would never be able to repay. When she had lost her first baby while protecting me, I thought our friendship would never be the same. I was so wrong. Instead, it brought us closer than I had thought we could ever be.

"No, Angel, thank you. You are an amazing friend and will be an amazing aunt. I want my daughter to know how much you mean to me. She will grow up to know how strong her Auntie Angel is. You have been there for me, through thick and thin, and I owe you my life. She would not be able to exist, if it wasn't for you, because I wouldn't be here to give her life. She will grow up to know all of that." She hugged me back, and turned to go inside as our husbands walked back into the room through the front door.

I grudgingly said my goodbyes to the twins, even though I knew they were in great hands with Shelly. This was the first time I would be away from them, and it scared the hell out of me.

After everyone went their separate ways, Donovan and I went for a walk down the beach. It felt like it did the last time we were here. As he reached over to hold my hand, I still had the same butterflies I did the first time he did it.

"Shelly and Cory are having a girl," I said. "They are naming her after me. Angela will be her first name."

"Wow, babe. That's great. I couldn't think of a better person to name a child after," he said. I blushed.

"Thank you."

"No thanks needed, my love," he said with a smile that melted my heart. We continued to walk, the waves trickling over our feet. I stopped, suddenly.

"You know, I was thinking… Isn't it crazy, the last time we were here, it was for the worst possible reason," I said as I wrapped my arms around his side. "But I am so thankful for that time we had here. Does that sound bad? That we have Abe to thank for us being together today?" I was talking more to myself at that point than I was to Donovan.

"Now that you mention it, I agree with you. I hate to admit I am thankful for anything that asshole did, but I am. I just wish you wouldn't have had to go through any of the bad stuff for us to end up as happy as we are now," he said as he kissed the top of my head.

"Me too," I whispered. I decided then, that we had walked enough. I wanted, no I needed, to get my husband back to our room, so I could show him how happy I was. I knew I didn't have to prove my feelings to him, but I wanted to show him anyway. Plus, I needed to do something to get my mind off of the absence of my children. Donovan would easily be able to do that. And he did…

Once we finally wore ourselves out from passionate love making, we lay beside each other in bed, breathless. Donovan reached over and pulled me so my head lay on his chest. His steady heartbeat was lulling me to sleep.

"I just can't believe how lucky I am," he said, the words rumbling in his chest.

"Hmmm?" I mumbled. I loved it when he spoke while I lay on his chest.

"Shelly is right, you know. I am the luckiest man in the world. I have the job I have dreamed about my whole life, two adorable and healthy sons, and an amazing wife." I lifted my body up on my elbow and rested my head in my hand. I looked him in the eyes, which were filled with wonder.

"We are both lucky, babe. Not very many people can say they

have found their soul mate, like we have. We may have had to go through some tough times before we were able to cross paths, but we did it. We have overcome every obstacle thrown our way. There is no other couple who is more meant to be, than we are." He pulled me down for a kiss and tucked my head back under his chin.

"You're right. We are both lucky. I don't care what anyone says. You are the best thing that has ever happened to me,' he said. After a while, he was quiet. I listened to his breathing, realizing he had fallen asleep, leaving me alone with my contented thoughts.

For the longest time, I had a really hard time wrapping my head around the past couple years of our lives. There were many things I would like to have done differently, but there were also as many things I would not have changed at all. We had been through hell and back, that was for sure. We both had lost our parents at a young age. Then, there was human trafficking, being shot, psychotic ex-girlfriends, suicidal best friends, and finally, twins. Donovan and I had built our relationship on things that, others would most likely say, were unimaginable.

# EPILOGUE

I reached down and picked up the lemonade pitcher from the table in the front yard. Braxton, Brody, and Angela decided they wanted to have a lemonade stand to make some extra money for the fair that night. As I walked into the house, I caught a glimpse of two dark-haired boys, and one blonde girl, go dashing behind me. I smiled and headed on in.

"I'm pretty sure Donovan and Cory bought more lemonade than anyone else in the neighborhood," Shelly said as soon as she saw me. She snickered.

"Yeah, I am thinking you're right," I laughed along with her. As I was putting the pitcher in the refrigerator, the front door flew open.

"Mom!" I heard. I turned to see the tear streaked face of Brody running toward me. He ran into my arms, crying into my chest. I pulled him back so I could look at him.

"What's wrong, buddy?" I asked.

"Braxton pushed me out of the tree house and I hurt my arm!" he screamed.

"Let me see it," I coerced and he showed me. It was red and a little bit swollen, but it wasn't broken. That much I could tell.

I walked back to the freezer, and pulled out the ice cube tray. I grabbed a sandwich bag, filled it with ice, wrapped a towel around it, and set it on Brody's arm. "Go watch T.V. I'm going to go talk to your brother." Walking outside, I thanked my lucky stars Donovan hadn't built the tree house more than five feet off of the ground. Even though the twins were ten years old now, I was still overprotective of them both.

"Braxton!" I yelled into the back yard. I watched a head peek up through a window of the tree house. It disappeared again. "Braxton! Come down here, right now!" It wasn't long before a very forlorn Braxton, followed closely by a scared Angela, came down the short ladder, heads down.

"Yes, Mom?" he asked innocently.

"Why did you push your brother out of the tree house?" I asked, sternly.

"He didn't, Aunt Angel. Brody fell out," Angela whined. She always defended Braxton. They were very close. Brody and Angela were close as well, but they didn't share the same bond as she and Braxton did.

"Is this true, Braxton?" I asked. He looked up, nodded, tears falling.

"He was on the window edge, playing around. I told him to stop, that he was going to fall, but he wouldn't listen. Then, he wasn't there anymore." He shrugged. "I ran to see where he went, and that's when I saw him running to the house," Braxton explained.

"It's true, Aunt Angel," Angela said, again, backing him up.

"Okay. Well, he said that you pushed him. He hurt his arm, so he is going to stay inside for a little bit. You two need to be careful. No one is to go in the windows, ever again. Got it?" I asked, looking from Braxton to Angela. They both nodded vehemently.

I walked back to the house and went into the living room.

Brody had the ice sitting on the arm of the couch and was laughing at something on the television.

"Well, it looks like you are feeling better," I said as I approached him. He jumped and hurriedly put the ice back on his arm. I had to stop myself from laughing at him. He wasn't a good actor.

"It still hurts. Did you ground Braxton?" he asked.

"No, honey, I didn't. Both he and Angela said you fell out of the window," I coaxed, patiently. He sighed, extremely loud, defeated.

"They're right, I did," he said.

"Why did you lie?" I asked.

"Because I saw Braxton kiss Angela, and it made me mad," he said bluntly.

Oh... Braxton kissed Angela? Wow. Okay, calm yourself, Angel. These things happen.

"Braxton kissed Angela?" Shelly called from the doorway. She, unlike me, couldn't contain her laughter as she walked back into the kitchen. I followed her in. When we got there, we were met with Donovan and Cory. They both were staring, wide-eyed, at me.

"I think we may have a problem. Maybe not today, but someday. We need to keep a closer eye on the kids. No more tree house by themselves," I said to all of them. Donovan laughed, followed by Shelly, while Cory and I watched them. "What's so funny?" I asked them.

"You heard Brody. Braxton kissed Angela. Not Angela kissed Braxton," Shelly said, defending her daughter. She was right, of course. I needed to keep my eye on these boys from now on, especially when it involved girls. I laughed, too, as I thought about it. Cory was looking at us all like we had lost our minds. He wasn't seeing the humor in our little inside joke.

"Hello! Doesn't anyone else see a problem here?" he asked. "First, it's an innocent kiss, then... what?"

"Yes, Cory," Shelly said. "We know we have to watch them a little bit more closely, now. The part that is so funny is the story about the day Angel and Donovan found out they were having twins. There was a young girl in the waiting room…" She stopped and looked at me, winking, and then continued. "Anyway, this girl was very young, maybe seventeen or eighteen. She was alone in the waiting room and very pregnant. She looked as if she was going to be a single mother. Angel couldn't fathom the thought of having a girl, and having her face something like that. It's kind of an inside joke."

As she finished with her story, Cory was staring at her, half confused, and half in shock. He glanced at Angela, and then back to Shelly.

"Ugh…" he said as it all finally sank in. I watched as all of the color drained from his face, stifling the giggle that threatened to bubble out of me at any minute. It was as if it had just hit him how full his hands were going to be once Angela got older.

*Thank God I have my boys*, I thought.

**Shalene Shellenbarger** earned a degree in Psychology. As a survivor of domestic violence, she often speaks to college students about finding inner-strength when faced with a life or death situation. Shalene is a single mother of two sons and lives in Perrysburg, Ohio. This is her first book.

Printed in the United States
By Bookmasters